Flight of the
Wild Geese

Pemmican Publications gratefully acknowledges the assistance accorded to its publishing program by the Manitoba Arts Council, the Province of Manitoba – Department of Culture, Heritage and Tourism, Canada Council for the Arts and Canadian Heritage – Book Publishing Industry Development Program.

Printed and Bound in Canada.
First printing: 2009

Library and Archives Canada Cataloguing in Publication

Thompson, T. D. (Twila Dawn) 1953-
        Flight of the wild geese / T.D. Thompson.
ISBN 978-1-894717-51-9
        I. Title.

PS8639.H643F65 2009   jC813'.6   C2009-902320-2

**PEMMICAN
PUBLICATIONS
INC.**
Committed to the promotion of Metis culture and heritage

150 Henry Ave., Winnipeg, Manitoba,
R3B 0J7 Canada
www.pemmican.mb.ca

 Canadian Patrimoine
Heritage canadien

 Canada Council   Conseil des Arts
for the Arts   du Canada

 MANITOBA ARTS COUNCIL
CONSEIL DES ARTS DU MANITOBA
YEARS/ANS

 Manitoba

Flight of the Wild Geese

T.D.Thompson

To the ones who kept on believing and encouraging: Eric, Doug, Mike & Jen.
Thank you with all my heart.

CHAPTER ONE

*T*HERE'S A PLACE where the foothills are a rolling gold-brown, the colour of the well-worn deer-hide Dad tosses on my bed for warmth in winter. The hills rise in slow gentle swells to cradle the Rocky Mountains to the west.

It isn't unusual in our area for temperatures to sink to -40 in January and soar to the +30 range in summer, but this was only mid-November and already it was so cold school had been cancelled for two days in a row.

On the day my life swerved off-course the thermometer had settled in at around -34, our high for the day here in White Plains, and the world outside the kitchen window was a ghostly snow-white. It was pretty, all that hoarfrost hanging on the trees like white icing – pretty as long as you didn't have to be out in it. The frost in the air magnified every brittle sound in a creepy way that made it awful satisfying to stay in a nice warm kitchen and doodle in the margins of my chemistry note-book. Our house felt more alone than ever though, situated as it is a half-mile from town on a dead-end road, and now it was like an island in a white sea.

White Plains is one of those little dots on the map. It sits on a forgotten stretch of old pitted highway where the prairie meets the foothills, and nobody comes here unless they're lost looking for a cutline to go hunting in the fall. People live here either because they have relatives on the reserve or because they just couldn't handle living in the city for one reason or another. And a lot of us don't welcome strangers very easily.

A few years back a stranger, an older guy, a white man, came to town thinking he'd open a little grocery and fit right in. He brought his nephew with him. The kid came from Toronto, and to prove a point he tried to start something after school at the baseball diamond. He called me 'Gandhi'. Got Indians and Indians mixed up, I guess. When everyone stopped laughing he went home. They moved away one night.

In the frozen netherworld that afternoon I could hear the footsteps thudding and squeaking their way through the packed snow on the road long before I realized they were heading for our place.

"Hey! Hey, c'mon!"

The school boxing coach believes in lots of long-distance running to keep in shape, and I'd heard that little quaver of Jamie's often enough in training to recognize it now even from a distance. His lungs are in terrible condition.

"Hey, you guys, open up!" Jamie's mittened fists were pounding on the door before I could get up from the table.

"Mr. Beaton! Hey, Dave! C'mon man, open the door."

Dad came out of the back bedroom and we both reached for the knob at the same time. In the split-second it took before we got the door open there was his expression of startled confusion, mixed with something else, something sinister and a little scary, a look I still see some nights when the dreams turn bad. It was like he already knew something, and for whatever reason, he was keeping it to himself.

We yanked the door back and Jamie Little Buffalo stumbled through the opening as if he'd been ready to bulldoze his way into the house if he had to. Les was behind him, struggling up to the house from the main road.

"She's back there." Jamie threw himself into a kitchen chair and bent over double so his head was lower than his knees. "Back there," he grunted. "Call the cops."

"Who's back where?" Dad asked.

Les staggered in through the open door, his dirty navy pea coat frosted over with moisture from the heat he'd lost in running. He was coughing up the cold air, and wiping the ice from around his mouth and nose. He looked pale and sick.

Frost clouded through the door behind them before I reached out and slammed it shut again.

"What's going on, boys?" Dad stood with his hands on his hips. "Who's back where?"

"Call the cops, man. I don't know who she is." Jamie put his arms on the table and shoved his face down into them.

"It was awful," he mumbled. "I thought it was just some old clothes somebody threw out. I was gonna put on the hat and scare Les."

"You thought what was some old clothes?" I wasn't following any of this.

"Her. The lady out there." Jamie swallowed hard and put his head back down.

His voice was muffled. "I pushed at the clothes. She's frozen solid. Just like a side of beef."

"Where?" I'd been outside earlier making a quick trip to the little grocery in town and I hadn't seen anything.

"In the ravine." Jamie lifted his head and kept it up this time. "Oh, man, it was creepy. I've never been so shook up in my whole life."

I couldn't help being suspicious. Any second now I half-expected both Jamie and Les to burst into their awful hee-haw laughs. Those two have reputations for being jokers of the worst sort since their idea of hilarious is usually pretty predictable and only funny to themselves. Tying knots in the boxing coach's gloves and putting lime Jell-O in his jockstrap, that kind of thing. People put up with them because they're basically harmless. I could tell the same kinds of thoughts were running through Dad's mind. He looked pretty dubious as he reached for the phone.

It was the look on Les's face more than anything else that made the difference in believing them or not. Les was green under his winter pallor. He looked like he wanted to throw up if he hadn't already got rid of everything in his stomach on his way up to the house.

"Hi, Pete," Dad was saying into the receiver. "Mike Beaton here. It's a freezer out there today, isn't it?"

He stopped for a minute and then laughed and shook his head and I knew, without him telling me, it was at another of Pete's Popsicle jokes. Pete has an endless supply of them, all goofier than the one before, normally having some relation to hardened male anatomy of one variety or another. It seems to be some sort of requirement for anyone in his career, because even the other guys he works with tell the same jokes.

"Listen, Pete," Dad said, "I've got a couple of kids here who claim there's something in our ravine your people need to come and take a look at."

There was another short pause. Dad was obviously reluctant to give out the information. "Well, actually it's Jamie Little Buffalo and Les Stevens."

There was an even longer pause and Les grinned weakly across the table at me. Some of his colour was returning.

"Well now, Pete, I know that." Dad was working hard to be reassuring. "I realize that, Pete, but I don't think they're kidding this time."

Pete's voice could be heard coming staticky over the line. "I remember the portable john parked on top of your Jeep, Pete, who could possibly forget?" Dad frowned at the wall. "No, no, I take full responsibility. I'm sure they saw something out there. OK, then. OK, see you soon."

Dad hung up and turned to face us, hands on hips and a frown on his face. "You boys better not be trying to pull a fast one on me . . .," he began.

He looked closer at Jamie. Normally neither he nor Les can keep a straight face. Now both of them looked sick and exhausted. Les seemed close to tears.

"You just better be telling the truth," Dad finished on a lame note.

CHAPTER TWO

$\mathcal{A}$ N HOUR LATER the driveway and the road running past our gate were lined with police cruisers and emergency vehicles.

First there had only been Pete's car, and he hadn't even bothered turning off the engine because he'd been so sure this would turn out to be another of Les' and Jamie's dumb tricks. After scrambling down into the ravine behind Jamie, though, he'd come back to his car radio and called in the troops. It looked like a set from a third-rate movie out there. The place was crawling with guys in uniforms and their dogs.

After a couple of hours and about six pots of coffee they turned off the rotating lights on their cars and just left the one at the end of the drive and one on the road revolving slowly in their red-blue, red-blue waves of light to warn drivers out in the dark to slow down and watch where they were going. Because our road dead-ends at the river past the old Connor place there hadn't been much traffic to warn. The road only gets busy in summer when guys take truckloads of friends and sometimes some girls down to the river at night for parties. Nobody parties outside when it's this cold.

In November the sun drops behind the trees early. The slow undulation of the lights in that mid-afternoon frozen grey light gave a sad kind of feeling to the dusk. It was getting colder, too. There was a build-up of hoarfrost on the insides of the windowpanes now. Last night had been about -40 and tonight showed signs of getting even colder. The wind had picked up, tossing small hard pellets of icy snow at the house.

Pete Bigbear came stomping into the kitchen around dinnertime. Jamie and Les were down at the station answering questions and Dad and I had just begun eating some warmed-over stew from the night before. Usually I give Dad a quick rundown of my day during the meal, but tonight he didn't ask and I didn't have the heart to begin. We were both thinking of that frozen body in the ravine. Our ravine. At least I figured that was where his mind was at. With Dad it's hard to tell. I'm used to how he is, but it's easy to see why other people can think he's sort of odd and how that thinking reflects back on me. There's no way of explaining him to anybody. All I can do is shrug, and I've made that shrug into a sort of art form, so I didn't ask him what he was thinking or try to tell him what was on my mind, either.

"Here." Dad jumped up at the sight of Pete, and poured an extra cup of coffee. "Want some pie?"

Dad's a great cook. He makes our bread and he bakes a lot of pies. Those are only two of the things that make him stand out around here. The rest are basically things that don't really bear mentioning. Things that are just a part of his personality, things he's picked up through the years. His famous silent spells for one. Those have been known to drag on for weeks at a time, where the most he does is grunt a yes or no – and then only if the questioner absolutely insists on an answer from him.

Even on good days, he's not the most communicative guy. At least not to me. Maybe he talks to Pete sometimes, and if he does he doesn't tell me about it, but mostly he's a listener. A lot of the time he's lost out there in some world of his own, the world he seems to prefer to the one living here in the house with me. Me, I don't care. Maybe it's better than having an old man who wants to tell you every little detail and expects the same in return.

The fact he's brought me up completely on his own from when I was real little, with no help from any extended family of women, is another of those outstanding traits, although Jamie's old Aunts more or less adopted both of us way back after Mom left, without seeming to care one iota whether Dad liked it or not. Over time, their input in our lives has slowly diminished, until now their role seems to be more that of self-proclaimed witnesses who keep an eye on whatever Dad and I are up to. Back in the early days, I remember them being a lot more active in my life. They seemed to like me better when I was really little, when they could tell me stories and I'd actually listen.

This informal adoption measure on the part of the Aunts seems to have Jamie half-convinced he's related to me or something. He tends to act like he's some kind of distant cousin, the kind that, if you were lucky, you'd only see once in 10 years at a funeral. The kind you'd be sort of glad to talk to for a while, if only to reassure yourself of what a bunch of total jackasses your long-lost relatives really were, thus confirming your initial impression of them. Even though I've hung with him since we were little, I don't get him confused with a relative. To me he's basically just another guy from school – a fact that seems to be lost on him most of the time.

Jamie's like a lot of kids here in town and on the reserve, whose biological parents have simply disappeared into the middle distance somewhere. If anyone even knows for sure who Jamie's parents once were, or where they went, they haven't been talking to Jamie. From all I can tell, not that I really care, he's completely content living with the Aunts and has blanked out any natural curiosity about the two people who made him in the first place. The Aunts took him when he was just a baby nobody seemed to want and they're the only family he's ever known.

Pete pulled a chair up to the table and accepted the pie with a nod of thanks. He hung his big fur hat on the corner of it, grabbed the coffee and tossed me a smile. He dropped his gloves onto the floor, rubbed his hands to get the blood moving in them again, then wrapped them around the hot mug.

"So." Dad seemed to be striving hard for nonchalance. "What's going on out there? What's the story?"

"No story." Pete lopped off a huge hunk of pie and chewed slowly.

"Man." He shrugged his arms out of his parka. "Man, I hate cases like this."

Pete shivered violently as some of the heat from the kitchen crept through all the layers of clothes he was wearing.

"It's awful cold out there," he said.

Pete's a big guy, taller than Dad, with huge shoulders and a chest like a line-backer, but the cold always seems to penetrate right to his bones. Dad is muscular in a lean, stringy way, but he's not very big. He's only average height and he doesn't weigh much more than I do, but he can outstay a guy like Pete when it comes to blizzards and freezing weather anytime. He doesn't seem to feel the cold.

"Who is she, Pete?" Dad's voice was real quiet. I think even then he had some kind of gut feeling he already knew the answer; he was just waiting for the official word.

Pete looked straight at Dad. He's not the kind of guy to pull any punches, but at the same time he's careful. A personality trait he's learned on the job.

"I don't know for sure, yet. Nobody knows for certain, but the body's about the right age. If it's her though, she's sure changed a lot."

His voice trailed off into silence and he sipped slowly at his steaming coffee. "We won't know for certain until the guys in the lab get some fingerprints and stuff."

"Yeah." Dad got up and poured Pete another cup of coffee. "Sorry to put you on the spot like that."

As far as I knew there was nobody from around here who had gone missing in a while, although deaths from the severe weather happened nearly every year, usually after somebody drank too much, forgot how cold it was outside and settled down for a little snooze in a snowbank. Or when somebody decided to show his girlfriend how tough he was and took an icy turn too fast.

People talk about poker faces, about eyes that don't give anything away, and Dad's face is just like that. It can look like a mask sometimes, when he wants to keep things to himself. His eyes get darker and go kind of flat and his mouth settles into a narrow line, the grooves on either side deepening. He was looking that way now and I couldn't tell what he was thinking.

Sometimes I wish I were more like him. I look like my mother. I have her black hair and eyes; I can see that much from the old photographs Dad has in an album at the back of his dresser. According to him I have her way of talking too, and it's impossible for me to hide anything from anyone, even teachers who hardly know me. What Dad doesn't seem to clue into is that I'm also a little like him; I don't trust people very easily, including him sometimes, and I'm real careful who I chose to be friends with.

From the little bit I've heard about my mother I think she used to talk a lot about her feelings and other people and what they were up to, and I can imagine how Dad's long silences must have weighed on her. They don't bother me much because I'm used to him. For as long as I can remember it's only been the two of us. A newspaper article about his paintings once referred to him as 'cerebral,' but after enduring one of his famous week-long silent spells I sometimes think cerebral is only a polite way of saying 'mental.'

Mom left when I was little. I was so young I'm not sure if I really remember her or if my memories are only dreams and bits of things Dad told me. He used to show me pictures and he'd talk about her once in a while and tell me how much she loved me, but it never seemed real. If she'd been so wild about me and loved me so much, then how come she'd just walked out on me?

Actually, she'd walked out on both of us. Just left a note on the kitchen table for Dad. He always told me he burned it, but a couple of years ago when he was out and I was snooping around looking for my Christmas presents I found it. It's in a little box on the top shelf of his closet, behind some old socks. It was real short and the writing was hard to read. 'Dear Mike,' it read, 'I have to go. Let me go. Take care of Davey,' and she'd signed it 'Marie.' Not 'love, Marie,' or anything, only her name.

I'm the Davey she mentions, but nobody calls me that anymore. All my friends call me Dave and teachers call me David, but up until I was three my mother called me Davey. That was a long time ago. I'm nearly 16 now, practically grown up, but once in a while if I'm really down about something I think I can actually remember her. I can almost feel her. She's tall and warm and she talks quietly about stuff I can never quite make out.

The look on Dad's face made me think he was remembering her right now too, but I knew he wouldn't actually break down and talk about her. Not to me, anyway. He hasn't mentioned her name in years.

CHAPTER THREE

I T WASN'T ANYTHING Dad came right out and said that got me thinking about who might be lying out there in the snow. It was more the look on Pete's face whenever he happened to glance over in Dad's direction. He'd be drinking his coffee, listening to Dad, and then he'd get carried away by the whatever they happened to be talking about, and sort of forget what he was doing, and then his eyes would settle on Dad's face for a split second before he'd almost jump out of his chair in his desperation to look over at me or the floor or the wall or anything, other than Dad.

It was starting to sink in just who Dad and Pete figured had died out there in the ravine. My hands suddenly felt cold and sweaty at the same time.

"How long will the lab guys take?" I asked.

Dad glanced over at me, but he didn't say anything. He pushed his chair back and went over to lean back on the fridge.

Pete cleared his throat and took another swig of coffee. "With a little pressure, the results could be here in a couple of days. Depends on a lot of things," he said.

"Like what?"

"Teeth. Dental records, if we need them. How up to date the records are and how badly decomposed the body is and things like that. We're not sure how long she was out there . . ." His voice dwindled into silence and he stood up.

"Look, I've got to get back to work." Pete shrugged his way into his coat and pulled his hat down over his ears. "Listen, Mike, try to carry on like normal. Thanks for the pie."

He slapped one huge paw on Dad's shoulder and tossed me a half-hearted wave. "Talk to you boys soon," he said as he went out the back door.

Pete was as good as his word. He must have put more than a little pressure on the guys in the city, I realized later when I had time to think about it, because he was back late the next afternoon.

Dad and I were home as usual. I was finishing off some homework at the kitchen table and Dad was in the little bedroom he uses as a studio. He was starting a new commission someone from an oil company in Calgary had asked him to do – a prairie scene for their head office.

Dad's paintings aren't what you'd expect from some guy out in the middle of nowhere. He uses strange colours and he throws in odd things a person doesn't expect to see in a painting, but those odd things, along with the angles he uses, make the paintings even more real. For example, there might be a beautiful healthy brook trout flopping faintly in the middle of a dusty prairie, or the skeleton of a dinosaur might be barely visible in the outline of a mountain range. He says he tries to get inside the mountain or the prairie and feel what it would be like to be those things, to live their history. Sometimes his pictures are so strong they just about jump out of the canvas at you.

Our house overlooks the ravine and the mountains in the far distance, and Dad does most of his sketching right out there on the back porch. It's real pretty and it's nice to be apart from the little town here, although everything is still within walking distance if you don't mind walking.

It used to be nice, especially when the weather was good, to walk through the ravine, then cut up in back of the school. It made the distance a little longer to use the ravine, but it was worth it. There are always birds and squirrels to watch. Now, the ravine wasn't just woods anymore; it had a more sinister status as the place where they'd found her.

Pete stood awkwardly just inside the kitchen door and waited for Dad to come out to join us. His silence was enough confirmation of whom they'd found. Dad put his arm loosely around my shoulders, his hand barely grazing my arm.

"It's her, Mike. It's Marie, all right." Pete glanced down at the puddle of melting snow collecting around his boots. "She ended up out there in the middle of that last heavy snowfall. It was awful cold."

"How did she die?" Dad's voice came out calm and clear through the buzzing that filled my head. Everyone seemed to be far away right then, a little echoey, as if they were talking through a heavy damp fog.

"Hypothermia. She froze to death." Pete took a chance and looked up again. "I'm sorry, Mike. Real sorry."

"Yeah, I know." Dad sat heavily in one of the kitchen chairs and rubbed his hand over the stubble on his chin.

"Guess I'd better shave," he said slowly, "if I'm going into town."

"Now, there's no real need, Mike. Wait until they get her cleaned up a little. The funeral home . . ."

"Funeral home!" Dad stood so suddenly his chair bounced backward onto the floor. "She's not going to any fancy funeral place, Pete. She's coming back out here to her real home."

"Well, sure." Pete put out a calming hand. "Of course you'll bring her back here. Everybody knows that, but she looks pretty bad right now, Mike, and the people at the funeral parlour know what to do to make her look a little bit better, that's all."

"I don't want her looking better." Dad practically spat the words out while he grabbed his jacket from its hook near the door. "I want her looking real."

He jammed his hat down over his head. "Come on, Pete, let's go!" he ordered, slamming his way through the back door.

Pete looked over at me.

"It's OK," I said. "Go with him."

"You all right?"

"Yeah, sure, I'm fine." Why wouldn't I be? I hadn't even known the woman. It all just took a little getting used to, that's all.

Pete still seemed reluctant to leave. "We'll be back as soon as we can, Dave. Your Dad just needs some time. I'll take him into town and make sure he gets back here tonight, OK?"

"Sure. Fine."

I knew Dad would be sitting out there in the police cruiser steaming mad and ready to take on the whole funeral industry if he had to. Dad's a quiet man until he gets riled up, and then he makes up for his quietness by jumping around and roaring like a bull moose with an attitude.

It also occurred to me that in this kind of weather Pete had probably left his car running so the engine wouldn't have time to get cold on him again. In Dad's current frame of mind it probably wasn't a very good idea to leave him out there in a running car, even if that car did happen to belong to the RCMP, and I guess that thought crossed Pete's mind right about then, too.

"Gotta go, Dave!" Pete shouted as he leaped through the back door.

Before it even banged shut behind him I heard the unmistakable growl of a car shifting from park into drive and I knew Pete was in for some exercise. It wouldn't be easy catching up to Dad in those heavy boots Pete was wearing, especially with the head start Dad had.

When I got to the front window to catch the action Pete was cutting a diagonal path through the snow, hoping to cut Dad off where the driveway turned onto the county road. Even from the house I could see his face redden from exertion and anger, his hands gesticulating wildly at Dad when he forced the driver-side door open and shoved his way into the car.

CHAPTER FOUR

THE DAY OF THE FUNERAL was downright miserable – cold, snowy and windy. Not many people showed up at the church and even fewer made the trip out to the graveyard.

The Aunts were there, of course, standing on either side of Dad and me. It was kind of comforting having Edith's hand on my shoulder through the service. Even Jamie seemed to sense the despair hanging over our house during those long cold days and kept his visits to a minimum. For his part, Dad had been even quieter than normal since his trip to town with Pete. Seeing my mother in the funeral home seemed to have drained his anger, and left only a brooding silence.

"She may have been on her way back here," Pete had told me that night after he returned with Dad. "Maybe she wanted to give it another try, or maybe she was on her way to somebody else's place and she just got lost. We'll never know."

The television was on, throwing a flickering light through the room. I wasn't watching it. I was curled on the couch, stiff from not moving. I'd been sitting there staring at the tube since Dad left, but nothing had registered. I had the sound turned down so the canned laughter wouldn't drive me nuts, and the actors looked weird and phony with only their lips moving and their faces registering all kinds of contrived emotions.

Pete and Dad dove into the house around 11, with a cold gust of wind tossing a few flakes of snow at their backs before they got the door slammed shut again. They stomped their feet, knocking clumps of snow from their boots and coats before crossing the kitchen floor.

Dad took a quick look into the living room, checking my whereabouts, before heading off down the hall to his own room. He didn't say a word, and I wondered if he'd been that quiet all evening or only after seeing her. I wished he'd come in and talk to me, tell me what happened. It was a fine time, I thought, for him to go into one of his famous silent spells.

It was beginning to look like I'd never find out what was going on, and then Pete wandered slowly into the living room with a coffee from the pot I'd been keeping hot on the stove, and sat down in the other chair. He was as quiet as Dad had been. He sat there, staring off into space, taking small sips of the hot coffee, not saying a word.

The whole thing was starting to royally piss me off. Did they think I didn't care? She had been my mother after all, and even though part of me didn't want to know what had happened, another part of me was grieving for her even if I didn't really want to grieve. When I was a little kid I'd gone to sleep thinking of her some- times, dreaming that when I woke up in the morning she'd be there in the kitchen making breakfast just like the TV families. Now, that would never happen.

"How did she look?" I knew it would have to be me to break the silence and that fact only fuelled my anger. Was I so unimportant these two big strong guys couldn't bother to overcome their own feelings long enough to talk to me?

"She looked better," Pete said slowly. "Better than she did yesterday."

"Was Dad pretty shook up?"

"Yeah."

"Did he recognize her?"

Pete nodded.

"Well, is he OK?"

"Yeah."

"Pete!" I almost yelled it. "Come on, man. What happened?"

Pete sighed deeply and took a long gulp of his coffee. He turned his eyes to the TV screen, but I knew he wasn't watching it any more than I was; it was only a way of keeping his eyes occupied and away from the pictures in his head.

"She might have been on her way here," he said finally. "It's a long shot at best, but I know that's what your Dad thinks."

Pete spoke slowly, obviously weighing each word. "What would have happened once she got here is another thing. She's been living a rough life and she's been living it for a long time. You can see it in her face." He shook his head. "Poor girl."

It looked like he was grinding to a halt again.

"Pete, please, I've got a right to know."

He took a long look over the rim of his cup, shook his head again, and put his feet up on the coffee table.

"I knew your Mom from way back," he began. "Long before she ever met your Dad. When he came along she was only 17, but she was already hitting the booze pretty hard. Living downtown, hanging around with a lot of different kinds of people – a lot of different men. She never could figure out who to trust and who to back away from. She had a tough life from day one on and she couldn't handle her own memories. She made a lot of mistakes."

He sipped at his coffee again. I was afraid to say anything in case it broke the mood. Nobody had ever really talked to me before about her. Dad was more reticent than normal whenever I tried to dig past the stories, all fake it sometimes seemed to me, about how much she loved me. Nobody else in town even seemed to remember her. And the Aunts, when I did manage to bring her name up, were so enigmatic and close-mouthed about her, they resembled two little native Buddhas more than the elderly women they actually were.

The only concrete information I'd been able to gather up over the years, I'd kept close inside where no one could get at it. It was like my own private stash of contraband. All I'd learned for sure was that she was born and raised on the Wolfwillow reserve about 400 miles north of here, the same reserve Pete had grown up on before he entered the police force and got stationed down here.

"What kind of mistakes?" I asked finally.

"You have to understand her folks drank pretty hard," Pete said, not answering my question. "For some people it's the way they were raised, it was a way of life and it still is. They didn't know any different. But people on booze are way different people than they are when they're sober. Especially if they drink all day, every day. They hurt inside then and that makes them hurt the people around them."

He stopped, obviously hoping I wouldn't want to hear any more, but I was hanging on to every word.

"Your Mom," he continued, "got treated pretty rough. There was no such thing as respect for kids in her folks' home and she didn't always get enough to eat. She used to come over to our house when she was just a wee little thing, dirty and tired and hungry . . ."

Pete shook his head and concentrated real hard on the cup in his hand. "My mother used to get a hot meal into her and put her to bed."

"How come your parents weren't drunk, too?"

Pete is full-blood Cree and proud of it. I think Dad is envious of him. Dad is a sort of born-again Indian. His ancestors are all European immigrants for generations back, but Dad has always had this idea that the Indians, before they were contaminated by white intruders, had lived ideal lives, just them and the mountains and plains and the spirits of their ancestors. When he talks about his beliefs it almost seems too perfect to be true, kind of like those tales of Camelot or Robin Hood. Maybe everyone needs some kind of dream to believe in.

In a way, I sometimes think he believes he was an Indian in a former life, and he's been stuck down here again in a foreign body with a foreign background. But at the same time, Dad's no hypocrite. He knows he's not native, and he has a special disdain for people who take on some Indian-sounding name and pretend to be something they're not. There are a few of those around – one old German guy, for example, who barely speaks English and calls himself 'Walks With Bear,' and who Jamie refers to as 'Digs With Gopher'.

Dad's always careful to make sure I know I'm part native but also part white. Beige, in other words. Tan. Not that it matters much around here. Everybody I know is part-something and part-something-else, except for the few that are pure white and there aren't many of them around. None of us is a pure-bred. We're not sled dogs; we're more your standard rez mutts from the pound. Pete, though, is the real thing and Dad's closest friend. Pete is descended from chiefs and warriors.

"My parents were more adaptable," he was saying. "They followed the old ways as much as they could, but they brought in the new ways too. They used the sweat lodge. We camped out a lot in the bush. Real camping, like in the old days. And my folks honoured their ancestors. That's important, too. And so in my house circum-stances were different."

Pete rubbed his nose hard with the heel of his hand. "I don't know," he said finally, "why some families work out and some don't. I see a lot of hopeless, hurting people every day, Dave, and they're every colour under the sun. Your Mom was one of the hurting ones."

All this new information wasn't easy to digest. I could almost picture my mother as she must have been when she was little, suffering through the kind of stuff that eventually made her the type of woman who would run from her own kid. It wasn't really all that hard to do. We don't live on the reserve and Dad isn't a treaty Indian the way he'd like to be, but my friends are Indian and white and a bunch of shades in between and I see plenty of the people Pete calls hopeless and hurting. White Plains is a real little town, the reserve is just down the road, and although I don't always know everyone around here personally, the whole area is small enough for most people to recognize everyone else at least by their last names.

In a way it makes the area like one big family, but families have their secrets and their old vendettas that go back for generations, and sometimes living here and talking to people can be like walking through a minefield blindfolded

"Where did she go when she left?"

"She was in Edmonton most of the time." Pete was getting quieter. "She lived in Edmonton. Downtown."

Then she'd only been a few hours' drive away. I'd been in Edmonton lots of times, but I'd never seen her. We'd never tried to find her.

"How come you didn't bring her back if she was only that far away? Why did you guys just let her go?"

Pete put his cup carefully on the table and crossed his burly arms over his chest. "Not that simple, Dave." His voice held a note of warning.

"Yes, it is! Sure it is!" I admit I was probably a little overexcited. "You just go there and find her and bring her home again."

I could hardly believe it. I'd always assumed she'd been far away, in Vancouver or New York or something. That nobody had a clue where to find her, because, of course, if Dad or Pete had known where she was they'd have gone to get her and everything would have been all right.

"He could have stopped all this from happening!" There was a sour taste in the back of my mouth. "She didn't have to die out there all by herself. She froze to death, Pete; she froze to death a half-mile from her own house! How could Dad let that happen?"

"Now, listen!" Pete glared down his long crook of a nose. "Wait just a minute, Dave! Your Dad loved that girl. He was nuts about her."

He paused for a long moment, obviously trying to decide how much to tell me. "Maybe he loved her too much, tried to protect her too much. She couldn't live up to his expectations, or maybe her past got in the way, I don't know." The words were bursting out of him now like bullets.

"She couldn't let go of her past life. It haunted her in a way I hope you'll never understand. There were things that happened to her back before she met your Dad that she couldn't forget. It's complicated, Dave. It's not something that can be solved just like that."

"What kind of past life are you talking about?"

"Look, Dave," he said forcefully, "everybody walks their own path in life. They make their own choices and their own mistakes. You can't choose that path for them; you can't erase the past or make things disappear if you don't like what happened. Your Mom chose to leave here. She chose her own path."

Pete stood and started pacing the living room.

"Your mother never really knew love until she met Mike. By then she was too far gone. She didn't know how to accept love and she didn't know how to give it, either. She was too scared, too wounded . . ."

"He could have fixed it." I couldn't shake the idea that Dad was somehow to blame for her leaving. "He could have been patient and waited for her to learn."

"Mike is the most patient man I know," Pete broke in, "but there are some things you can't do for other people no matter how badly you want to. He tried, Dave, I know how hard he tried, but people have to do it themselves and sometimes they can't find the way."

"Oh, come on, Pete!" There was a lump in my throat making it hard to swallow, but I just couldn't let it go. "She could have stayed if he'd let her."

"She left him, remember? There were things going on in her life even he didn't know about. Things she kept secret from everyone. Things people still don't know about. Your Dad was trying to protect you. He's still trying to protect you. When you get mad at him, think about being a dad yourself someday. Think about some things you might not want your kid to know."

Pete stopped pacing in front of me and sat down on the edge of the coffee table so he could look me straight in the eye while he talked. I had a strong feeling he still wasn't telling me everything he knew, but only bits and pieces, just the parts he thought I could handle. It was infuriating.

"Your Mom was on alcohol and pills when she left here," he said gently. "She tried to clean up. She went to the band council centre, she went to the doctor, but none of it did any good. She left here because she needed the booze and the dope and she didn't want to drag you into it. She did that much for you anyway! She didn't want you living her kind of life. It nearly killed your Dad."

So there it was, neatly laid out for me. Mom left home to give me a better life, but my life wasn't better. Dad stuck around because somebody had to look after me. Maybe he wanted to follow her, but he couldn't; he was trapped.

"How'd she live? Did she work somewhere?"

Pete stood and walked to the bookcase. He obviously wasn't going to answer and his silence told me more than words could have. I suddenly had a very clear idea of what my mother had done to stay alive in the city.

"I'm going out."

I stood up fast and went for my coat. My eyes were so blurry I could hardly see the hook it was on and I had to feel for my boots with my feet.

"Come on, Dave, don't go out in weather like this." Pete's voice was gruff. "She loved you. If she hadn't cared it wouldn't have hurt her to think of you growing up embarrassed by her."

"I wouldn't have been embarrassed." I swiped a hand across my face. "I'd have helped her. I wouldn't have been like you guys!"

One arm was in the sleeve and I was groping around with the other one, trying to find a way in. "I could have looked after her," I finished.

"Maybe you wouldn't have been embarrassed by her," Pete agreed gently. "Not at first. And maybe you could have helped her. But maybe she was humiliated by her own behaviour. She didn't want everyone in town seeing her and linking her to you."

Suddenly it all got to me – all Pete's preaching about Mom and how she felt. It was like he thought he was God or something and knew exactly what was going on inside everybody. It was too much.

"How do you know so much?!" I yelled. "What made you the God damn authority on all this stuff? You don't know a God damn thing about it, Pete! You're probably making it all up!"

"I visited her when she was drying out a couple of times," he said, quieter than ever.

I stopped searching for my sleeve. "You not only knew where she was all along, but you actually visited her? You knew and you didn't tell Dad?"

"Your Dad knew."

I rubbed my hands hard across my face and slumped down in the pile of boots by the back door. "He knew?"

"She wouldn't see him. She was on her own again by the last time. She'd left the other guy. He was a real bum, a real hard man . . ." Pete's voice trailed off and I had to strain to hear. "I talked to her a few times. I tried, Dave, I really tried, but she was too far down. I couldn't get through."

"On her own again? What do you mean 'on her own again?'"

And then suddenly all the fight went out of me, and so did all the questions. It didn't matter anymore. She wasn't coming back. She had been dead to me for years and she couldn't get any deader.

Pete sat down on the floor next to me and flung a heavy arm across my shoulders. I didn't even try to hold back the tears any longer. It didn't matter anymore if Pete saw me cry.

I knew he was hurting, too. I could hear it in his voice. Pete is a good cop, and it must have driven him crazy to watch the little girl he remembered his mother feeding throw herself down the tubes, knowing there was no way he could help her.

The funeral was two days later. Dad and I hadn't talked since the time we found out it was Mom in our ravine. Not really talked, anyway. He asked me what I wanted for supper and I told him who called while he was locked up in his painting room, but that was all.

We stood there on the windswept, snowy hillside after everyone else, including Pete, had left. Just stood there looking at the casket where it sat on boards laid over the hole in the ground. The snow around was trampled with footprints, but at least it was clean and white with a purity to it that made it pretty to look at.

It was so cold. I wished at least we could put her someplace warm. It seemed awful cruel, after she froze to death, to put her back into frozen ground.

Dad blew warm breath on his hands and rubbed them hard, then stuck them under his arms for warmth.

I felt like I'd been cold and shivering all my life and I'd never be warm again. I wondered if she felt the same. Maybe somewhere out there she felt the icy cut of the wind and longed for a way to get herself warm.

CHAPTER FIVE

A COUPLE OF MONTHS LATER we were mounted on horseback bound for Wolverine Lake.

Dad had been biding his time, silent and gloomy, and obviously focused on something outside of what was going on in our house, while Christmas and New Year's dragged past and then he'd suddenly become a man reborn. His theory, as far as I understood it, seemed to be that a person could return to his roots, or his wannabe roots in his case, and live life the way they did in the old days. Only that way, living off the land, surviving by our wits, could we again find peace.

Independent. Free. Wild and untamed.

"Starving!" Pete hollered. He watched Dad check the travois for the hundredth time. "Starving! Cold! Lonely!"

"And nuts," someone added cheerfully from the crowd that had gathered to see us off. Several heads nodded in agreement.

The weather had finally evened out to just below the freezing point, and I was seated, shivering both from cold and from nerves, on top of the tallest horse I'd ever had the misfortune to meet.

Never having been close enough to one of them to even pat it on the nose until a couple of weeks ago, I was having more than a little trouble getting used to the perspective from way up here. Not only that, but I was beginning to worry that motion sickness might get to be a problem. The animal beneath me seemed to move to his own internal temperamental sway, not unlike the heaving swells you might see in a *National Geographic* special about some poor insane schmuck who decides to sail by himself in a six-foot rowboat across the North Atlantic during typhoon season.

Ajax, my dauntless steed, seemed to have slept poorly the night before, no doubt in horsey anticipation of our journey, because he suddenly stretched out a long neck and bared huge yellowish teeth in a gigantic yawn that nearly pulled my arms out of their sockets.

I reached forward, hoping not to fall off and humiliate myself in front of all these people, and gave his neck what I trusted he would think of as a reassuring pat. He stretched again, tossing his head roughly from side to side this time, ending in a long dramatic shudder that rippled through his whole body.

While clutching at his mane in an awkward attempt to stay aboard I accidentally dropped a rein. It was the chance he'd obviously been looking for and he immediately stepped forward, planted one huge hoof on the fallen rein, and gave Dad a nudge in the seat of his jeans that nearly knocked him into next week.

"Dave!" Dad spun around and made a grab for the trailing rein. "Get control of your animal! Remind him of who's boss around here."

Well, I would gladly have reminded Ajax of who was boss, but I was afraid he already knew. And I didn't think Dad would find any comfort in having reality spelled out for him.

"Now listen, Pete." Dad was irritated, besieged from all sides, as he turned to face his friend. "We can do this. I know what I'm doing."

"OK, OK." Pete held up both hands. He face was tired and drawn and he looked more than a little worried. "But why do you have to take Dave out of school? And not only him, but Jamie? Why not just go off on your own for a little while and get back to normal and then come home? Or maybe just do something with them around here, like a fishing trip in the summer, or something? A nice fishing trip, Mike. Think about it, man – you could pitch a tent up one of the cutlines near a nice little stream, and . . ."

"Knock it off, Pete." Dad grunted as he tightened the girth on his own horse. "Hold up there, Stanley," he murmured when the animal started backing away. "Hold up, boy."

Stanley quieted right down and stuck a friendly nose in Dad's armpit. My father had never been on a horse either before this last week, but he'd had us both riding every morning in the field behind our house in preparation for the trip, and Stanley had obviously taken quite a shine to Dad over those few days.

Dad's never been a rule-follower. He's always gone his own way, and the day he showed up with the two horses in the back of a borrowed trailer I'd been taken off-guard but not overly shocked. Life now seemed to be divided into two sections: life before the funeral, when I still had a fighting chance of predicting what might take place each day, and life after. Life after was so far impossible to predict. I prefer predictability. I like to know what's going to happen so I can be prepared for it. This jumping from one kind of lifestyle into another was hard to take, but I was determined to give it my best shot. Dad was suffering, that much was obvious, and I wasn't about to make his load even heavier.

Besides, it wasn't like we'd never camped before. We'd gone on a few trips over the years, but mostly Dad and I car-camped. We'd pull up to a quiet spot near a creek on some little gravel back road and we'd throw a tarp over a tree limb and then tie it to the open car door for a kind of lean-to. I'd toss stones in the creek. Dad would draw. We'd eat what we brought with us and we'd leave our milk in the running water of the stream to keep it cold. Roughing it the easy way. We ate white bread and peanut butter. Not exactly chasing our food down, skinning it and then propping its carcass over a roaring fire, but we called it camping.

Once news of our expedition had reached him through the town grapevine, Jamie had insisted on coming along. He'd pleaded and begged until even Dad found it hard to hold out any longer. The day he'd showed up at the house riding a little runty mixed-breed pony he'd picked up for a couple of bucks somewhere Dad had been forced to give in. Now Jamie was sitting there at the edge of the crowd, crouched on board a sagging Sparky, both of them looking half-asleep, or half-frozen; it was hard to tell which.

This exodus from White Plains, from our house and our car and all the stuff Dad and I owned, now seemed a looming insanity. Kind of like jumping off a cliff to see what it's like to be an eagle. The jumping part might be close to the same feeling, but the difference would come on landing.

At one point, up until we'd saddled up this morning actually, I'd been almost convinced it could work. But now reality, as represented by the crowd of neighbours hanging around our yard, laughing and joking at our expense, was sticking its middle finger right in my face.

Nobody in their right mind would take this way of dealing with a death in the family. Or out of the family, depending on how you looked at it. Depending on how crude you wanted to be, or how heartless.

And nobody would put himself and his kid in mortal danger of freezing to death out in the bush just to satisfy some wild theory, some whim. Which led me to the logical conclusion that Dad had quite possibly gone crazy with grief or guilt. In which case travelling with a possible madman into the woods in the middle of winter on some wild quest for inner peace might not be the best idea. At least, those were the thoughts percolating uneasily in the back of my mind as we waited in the windswept yard for Dad to be ready to leave.

A few days back it had all seemed so simple. The way Dad explained it, we'd be living like the Indians did in the old times, and through that kind of simple lifestyle we'd find a way to deal with Mom's death and come out of it as stronger people.

"Listen, Dave." Dad's voice had been gruff and to the point when I'd tried to discuss the pros and cons of the plan with him. "Everybody in the old days lived like that. They thrived on it."

"Yeah, but Dad, this isn't the old days anymore," I'd started. "It's cold out there, it's snowy, there's . . ."

"Dave, there's nothing to be scared of. We'll just head out of town, up into the foothills, and find ourselves a place to set up camp. We'll find a good windbreak. We can hunt, and we'll bring dried foods. It'll be just the two of us alone in the bush, learning to rely on each other, trusting in nature for our survival. It will bring us closer together. We can share the experience."

By the time he got to the part about cleansing our souls and striving for purpose and peace, I'd pretty much tuned him out. The kind of life he'd always envisioned native tribes living back a few hundred years ago had always seemed a little hard to believe to me, but it was what he was aiming at finding now.

"Dave, we won't be out there forever," he'd reasoned a couple of days later, having obviously thought about it some more. "Just a month or two, maybe 'til spring, just long enough to get rid of the bad karma hanging over us." There was a tortured look in his eyes when he spoke, and that was when I'd fully realized we were really going to do this crazy stunt, and that no matter what he decided, I'd be there for him.

And then Jamie started dropping over at unexpected times, hanging around trying to give Dad a hand with the dishes and asking his opinion about stuff, in such an obvious and heavy-handed attempt to gain favour, I figured Dad was bound to see through it. All Jamie really wanted was a break from school, but by the time he got finished listing all the reasons he should be allowed to go along, leaning heavily on a core of native spirituality that he'd never referred to before, Dad had only been able to weakly insist the Aunts give their approval, probably figuring they'd be too smart to ever give it. Which turned out to be another misjudgment on his part.

Those old Aunts are a force to be reckoned with, and if he'd asked, I could have told him that before things got so out of control. They operate under their own set of rules and always have. Agendas mean nothing to them. The ordinary rules of human behaviour are like reading Sanskrit or something to the rest of us. They took Dad totally by surprise by not only agreeing to allow Jamie to go on the trip, but also by insisting on being included themselves.

They'd sat there in the kitchen in their jeans and sweaters, both little women comfortably stretching grey sock feet towards the warmth of the oven where Dad had a batch of bread baking.

"She makes good pemmican." Aunt Helen had nodded in Aunt Edith's direction. "Real good biscuits, too."

I was quiet, but I could see the skepticism on Dad's face and they did too, because Aunt Edith had chimed right in.

"She was a teacher aide. At the school." She bobbed a nod toward Aunt Helen. "She's a good teacher. She knows a lot. She can start a campfire with wet wood."

"Well, you know, I'd really only planned on David and myself," Dad began, hedging his way out of the situation.

"I can snare squirrels." Aunt Edith stated the fact as proof of her abilities. She looked him up and down carefully. "You ever skin a rabbit?"

"Well, no."

"Vegetarian?"

"No." Dad sounded defensive.

Aunt Helen nodded her head briskly. "We trapped with our old uncle. We lived in the woods all year in the old days."

"When we were girls." Aunt Edith's face broke into a wide grin, splitting her wrinkled features and turning her brown eyes up at the corners. "You need us. Be home in a week by yourselves. Everyone will laugh."

This whole concept still seemed barbaric to me, but I was kind of relieved at the idea of more people than just myself and Dad on this journey. I'm not much of a woods guy at heart. It always seems to me that they invented things like walls for a reason. Walls, a roof, flushable toilets. Although I do know a couple of old guys who still don't have indoor plumbing. They trek on out to the little one-seater or else just look for a bush whenever they need to go. I'll probably end up just like that. I'll be a grandpa thinking the latest gadget is a Wii and I'll start jumping around and my grandkid will be all abashed, saying, 'Grandpa, you don't need to do that anymore. The 'droids do it for ya.' Our cave-dwelling ancestors would probably laugh their heads off if they could see us heading out with our backpacks and dome tents.

The long, silent days after Mom's funeral and through Christmas had been busy ones for Dad. He'd thought it all out. He had lists of things we'd need – lists he'd pared down until only the barest of essentials remained. He had a whole saddlebag packed tight with nothing but books on survival, so at least I knew this wasn't some kind of suicide mission.

It was something he needed to do and, once he'd explained the concept to me about a dozen times and pushed and prodded a little, I was starting to see his point.

It was Pete who'd been impossible to convince.

"You guys are crazy!" He'd been unable to even sit still the night Dad and I told him our plans.

He crossed and uncrossed his legs and jumped around in his chair like there was a small electrical current running through it.

"Dave is going to flunk his year at school. Put your kid first, for crying out loud!"

"Dave will learn more where we're going than he ever would in school," Dad had said. "He'll learn about himself. He'll learn about life."

Pete made a noise of disgust. "If you could only hear yourself," he said. "You sound like a nutcase!"

"Thanks, Pete." Dad's voice was dry and cold.

"You know what I mean. A boy needs to be with his friends." Pete took in a big gulp of air and slowly let it out. "You need to be around people, too. It's no good cutting yourself off like that."

Dad seemed tired when he finally answered. "We're not cutting ourselves off." His voice had been nearly a whisper. "We're not trying to prove anything. We want to live another way of life, Pete, why can't you see that? A clean, pure way of life. This will be our new start."

Pete snorted his disgust.

"Out where the wild geese fly," Dad had added as an afterthought.

CHAPTER SIX

OLVERINE LAKE WAS a solid five days' ride from White Plains, first over a gravel road and then following hiking trails and cutlines, before cutting cross-country through the foothills and up into the high country.

Dad was impatient to get started. He jerked at Stanley's girth and paused to roll some of the stiffness out of his shoulders. He checked the packhorses one last time, tightening ropes, re-tying knots, going over every detail.

"You got some paper for drawing?" Aunt Helen rode up alongside. "You might need to draw."

Someone in the crowd guffawed and Dad shrugged. "No time for drawing out on the trail," he said.

Whatever meaning his art had held for him in the past seemed to be gone, at least for the time being. I couldn't remember a time when Dad hadn't been painting or sketching or dreaming up something new to work at. In his downtime from painting he'd always kept busy building frames and stretching canvases while his next project simmered at the back of his mind. He's always been the kind of guy to have about 10 things on the go at once. It was hard seeing him lost like this, with time weighing heavy on his hands. The magic that his art had always held for him had vanished, and now all his energy was funneled into one purpose. Maybe it was because he'd realized all the drawing in the world wasn't going to change it from a cold place where people die.

"Look after the house, Pete!" He swung up, and I saw him wince a little when his butt hit that cold saddle. "Everybody here?" He placed a hand on Stanley's rump and glanced back over the crowd. "Where's Edith?"

"She's coming." Aunt Helen was obviously unperturbed by her sister's tardiness. "She's bringing Lisa."

"Lisa? Who's Lisa?"

"You'll see."

"Now, listen." Dad's voice was harsh with tension. "We said we'd leave at exactly 10 sharp. It is now . . ."

"You should leave your watch here." Aunt Helen was quiet but firm.

"Now, Helen," Dad started. "This trip will be long and very tiring, particularly for the elderly." At this point he must have realized a major tactical error because he hurried to add, "Not that you are elderly. Actually, it'll be tougher by far on David and Jamie. The younger people are going to find this a real stretch. At any rate," he dwindled off, seeming to recognize a losing battle when he saw one, "it's time to get this show on the road."

Helen, who had simply gazed at him dispassionately through his fumbling speech, now said, "Here they come."

The crowd had separated slightly to allow Aunt Edith passage. She was seated like an ancient queen on top of an enormous white mule. Perched casually behind her on the animal's rump was a young woman, a girl really, maybe a little older than me, but still young enough she probably should have been at school. Her hands clutched the sides of Edith's coat, and at their side was an enormous shaggy grey dog.

The girl glanced down and whistled softly. The dog's ears picked up at the sound, and he whined slightly. She blew him a kiss.

"OK," Dad said. "Drop your passenger and let's get going."

At this point even I was starting to worry about getting our motley little group out on the trail before some of us, me in particular, chickened out altogether. Sitting on the sofa and watching a little TV had never seemed so tempting. But right in front of me the little drama continued as Dad made his first of what would become many face-offs with one or both of the Aunts.

"Lisa is coming." Aunt Edith sounded as though she wasn't prepared to argue the point any further. "She stays with us."

"She can't come." Dad was firm as he motioned toward the girl. "Get down."

"This is Lisa Buchinski," Aunt Edith said softly, "and she is coming with us."

"Let's go." Helen turned her horse and began leading the way out of the yard.

The packhorses were restive, stamping hooves in anxiety now that the animals in front of them were in motion, and after a long silent moment staring at the back end of Helen's horse as it walked away, Dad clucked in a strangled way at Stanley and began lining up the string of horses.

There was something really disturbing about this Lisa Buchinski chick. Her dark eyes settled first on Dad for a long analyzing moment, then me, before flicking away past us to her massive dog. Ignoring the exchange between Dad and Edith, she smiled down at her dog and tossed him another kiss.

I was trying to see Dad's face, get a reading on the situation, but he kept it turned to his pack string. The muskrat hat an old trapper had given him years ago hid most of his face, and with the flaps pulled down to protect his ears and neck from the cold he was pretty effectively camouflaged.

"We turn at the old path up to the beaver dam," Aunt Helen called back to us.

"No!" Dad said suddenly. He sounded desperate. "We have only enough food for the five of us. This has all been planned right down to the last detail. You must listen to reason! Please!"

Dad's never been the aggressive kind. It always showed in teacher interviews, when he'd sit there looking even more uncomfortable than me if that's possible, while some teacher threw his weight around a little and talked about applying myself and family influence and things Dad didn't want to think about. He was definitely uncomfortable now.

"In the old days we didn't make plans," Aunt Edith called over her shoulder.

Helen stopped her horse and turned to face Dad. "In the old days when a new member joined us we fed them. We didn't count how many."

The animals, with Jamie's aunts on top, moved down the drive and Stanley whickered softly after them.

Dad's face was grim, but he began to carefully steer himself and his packhorses through the knots of bystanders who still cluttered the yard.

Pete grinned, showing the first smile I'd seen on his face since the funeral. "See you fellows later," he said softly. "Make sure you don't do anything stupid."

The packhorses fell in step, testing their loads, as they trailed out of the yard and wound down the driveway. The horse at the end nipped with big yellow teeth at the rear of the animal in front of him. I held Ajax back, intending to keep my distance from any show of irritability on the part of the scrappy little packhorses.

Ajax tossed his head and danced a little, showing off and nervous at the delay, until I loosened the reins and let him follow the others. Jamie pushed his little horse into step beside me, waving his woolen hat back at those remaining behind.

"Who is she anyway?" I asked him. "Does Dad know her?" I didn't think I'd seen her around before and I was pretty sure I'd have remembered if I had.

"Who?"

"Auntie Edith," I said. A pointed bit of sarcasm, which was completely lost on Jamie.

"Sure you know her," he replied, aghast. "You've played Scrabble with her at my house!"

"Not Edith!" I snapped. "That girl with the dog. Why did she look at us so weird?" I was remembering the one and only sidelong glance she'd shot my way.

"Must be your good looks, man," Jamie sniggered. "She's probably in awe of your masculine hulk. Your sheer, manly presence. Girls are suckers for guys on horses. Never fails."

Jamie suddenly let loose with a high-pitched whoop that caught me off-guard and sent Ajax skittering madly off to the side.

"What're you doing, man? You're nuts, you know that?" My hands were shaking as I brought Ajax back in line again. It seemed a miracle I was still in the saddle and not dumped in some snowbank in front of all those nosy neighbours. "Why'd you go and do that, anyway?"

"I wish I had a real cowboy hat." Jamie's tone was wistful. He rested one hand on his animal's swaying rump and stared back at what was left of the crowd in our yard.

People were wandering away back home now, leaving our place with a forlorn abandoned look. Pete stood alone, watching us leave, and I threw him a last wave.

"If you were wearing a real cowboy hat," I said to cover the lump in my throat, "your head would freeze." I shivered and huddled a little deeper in my parka. "Your ears would freeze and drop off just like they do on cats that are out in the cold too long."

"Very funny."

"I'm serious."

"Jamie the Earless," he muttered, as if trying his new name out to see how it sounded. "I guess cowboys must have had earmuffs or something. Or ear transplants or rubber ears, maybe. Nothing to hear out there anyway in the old days. No radio. No TV. Just coyotes, maybe." He gave a rolling shudder and smirked at me.

The horses plodded along until we couldn't see the house at all, and Jamie finally grew silent and stopped mumbling about ears. He whistled an annoying little tune under his breath, but except for that and the creaking of leather saddles rubbing against ropes and blankets it was quiet. Only the sounds of the horses broke the stillness.

Ajax snorted deeply and coughed from way down deep in his chest as the cold air settled in his lungs. Horses were such a foreign element to me. I was suddenly certain they'd never survive in this cold. They'd all get pneumonia or something from lugging the weight of us, and all our provisions, up the side of a mountain. We'd be trapped up there in the wilderness with a bunch of dead horses and no way to get home.

Ajax coughed again, blowing his sides up dramatically and heaving out a cloud of white air.

On the other hand, I was also pretty sure some of these horses, mine in particular, knew more than they were letting on. Ajax seemed to have enough dramatic sense to be able to play sick in order to garner sympathy.

"Who's that girl, anyway?" I returned to my former topic, more for something to talk about than anything else. "Where'd she come from?"

"Just some stray the Aunts picked up," Jamie answered carelessly. "Like a million others. Some kind of cousin, or somebody's sister or something." He threw a lopsided grin at me. "They know her. She's OK. I dunno. Me, I try not to pay attention to them, otherwise they'd drive me nuts."

Too late to worry about that, I thought, since you're already way more than simply nuts. "What's she doing, coming with us? Dad had this whole thing planned down to the last detail and I don't think he's too crazy about her coming, too."

"He'll get over it." Jamie shrugged and wiped at his nose. A long squidge of liquid smeared on his glove. "Talk about something else," he demanded.

"Yeah, but what I can't figure out is why she'd ever want to come with us anyway." I just couldn't seem to let the subject drop. "This isn't going to be much fun or anything. In fact, it's bound to be cold and lonely and a lot of hard work. I still don't even know why you wanted to come with us, because even I don't want to be with us. Except I know you're half insane."

"She was at our house the last couple of weeks. She likes being outside." Jamie shrugged and shifted uncomfortably in his saddle. "Talk about something else," he insisted.

Normally Jamie is the kind of non-stop talker you just pray will shut up sometime, but now he was being even more close-mouthed than Dad. He was probably already bored and cold and mentally cursing his stupidity in coming with us, wishing he were home in front of a nice warm TV. It was an attitude I felt I could sympathize with.

"How'd she get out to your place? Do the Aunts know her or something?" I waited a minute, and when only the creak of saddle leather broke the silence, I added, "Man, what's the matter with you? You're way too quiet. You sick or something?"

"I'm reserved, man, that's why I don't talk much. Like your dad. I've got reservations. Get it, man? 'Reservations'? 'Reserved'? Get it?"

Oh, I got it all right. Only too well. "Shut up, Jamie."

I let the silence fall again. Jamie was obviously not interested in discussing the mysterious Lisa, and after the first bit of curiosity neither was I. What I'd seen of her so far was pretty uninspiring. She was bundled up in a goose-down parka that was so huge on her it might have fit Pete. Scarves, hats and gloves covered the rest of her. Only the glimpse of dark eyes and a fringe of black hair gave any indication there was an actual person hiding inside all those clothes.

It had been reasonably sunny and a little bit warmer while we were saddling up, but now the day was chilling down again. The wind picked up and gusted dry snow across the gravel road in front of the horses' feet.

"Traffic!" Dad hollered from several horses in front of Jamie and I. "Ditch, everybody!"

We reined over quickly, plunging the horses through drifts the road crews had left behind when clearing up from the last storm, and waited.

A couple of logging trucks hurled their way down the narrow road, spitting chunks of frozen gravel out from under their wheels. The first driver tossed a salute. The second tooted a long blast on his air horn. The horses went crazy at the noise, neighing with desperation and plunging wildly through the heavy drifts.

"Whoa! Hold on!" Dad shouted hoarsely. He was sawing away at his reins, desperately trying to keep Stanley out of range of the flailing packhorses.

The string of animals was rearing and jumping, tangling itself in the rigging. The more tied up the horses got, the more frantic they became, until their bodies were so knotted up in their lead ropes they could barely move. Dad's lips were moving in a silent swearing spree as he dismounted, landing hip-deep in snow, and flipped Stanley's reins over a willow branch.

While Lisa whistled softly for that big dog of hers, and the Aunts offered commentary, I personally felt it was safer to keep quiet.

"The big brown one is crazy," Aunt Edith observed calmly.

The animal she was referring to had reared up yet again in an effort to free itself. Part of the lead rope was hooked around a foreleg, holding it up at an awkward angle, and the pack had shifted until it hung nearly under the horse's belly.

"Might break that leg if it don't calm down," she continued.

Aunt Helen had reined her horse around to face Dad. "That one is even crazier."

She pointed a long forefinger at the horse pulling the travois. It had reared around and twisted itself in its rigging until it was nearly sitting on the load.

The Aunts bucked their mounts back up onto the hard gravel road and Lisa slid down over the rump of the mule. As she went she called to Dad to hand her Stanley's reins.

I slipped reluctantly down from Ajax, handed my reins to Jamie and slapped Ajax on the rear as Jamie led him up and over the ditch bank. My legs were instantly numb from the cold and my fingers were like sticks of wood as I went to help Dad. By the time we had the animals sorted out, calmed down and back up on the road again our jeans and long underwear were soaked through and stiff with cold.

"Take the saddle off Ajax," Dad ordered. "Tie it on Misty's load. You'll warm up and maybe even dry off a little riding bareback."

He looked exhausted, his face grim and drawn, as he turned to face the rest of our group.

"Anyone ready to quit?" His voice ached with exhaustion and something that sounded close to despair. "It's OK, just turn your mounts around and follow the road back. It's not far."

He faced each of us in turn. Nobody made a move.

"We turn off the gravel after the next bend," Aunt Helen said in a quiet voice. "Let's go."

She turned her horse and headed off down the road with Aunt Edith and Lisa right behind her on the mule. Dad's head sunk deeper into the collar of his coat. He heaved himself up on Stanley and clucked softly at his pack string, cajoling them into forming a crooked line behind him.

The heat from Ajax sent shivers up my spine as it penetrated the frozen jeans. Little clouds of steam began to rise from my legs. It felt like I was sitting on top of a furnace, and for the first time I sensed how a person could get emotionally attached to his horse. I reached forward and gave him a pat of thanks.

Lunch that day was cold biscuits and hot tea, and then we were right back into the saddle. Life had taken on a certain monotony, moving in rhythm to the horses' gaits, the creak of cold tack, the bothersome small details of getting a fire started and scooping up snow for tea. Already our lives back home seemed far away.

The cutline we followed angled off from the gravel road, making a long gradual climb up the side of a snow-beaten hill toward a jagged little trail that would take us farther from settled country and deeper into the wooded foothills.

The two old Aunts were still in the lead and Dad seemed content to just let them stay there. He looked happier now as he glanced back now and then to check out his pack string.

"How do you guys know about this place?" Jamie was eyeing the thick brush on either side of the cutline as if expecting to see the eyes of wild animals following our progress. I half expected the same thing. "What if we're headed in the wrong direction?"

"Pete showed me this place years ago," Dad replied. He flicked his reins playfully against Stanley's neck. "Years ago," he repeated as if to himself.

"Many moons," Jamie intoned in an aside to me. He laughed a short bark. "Long before the white hordes descended on our virgin shores. Long before the bearded ones entered our teepees. Long before . . ."

"Knock it off." I was tired and in no mood for kidding around.

The unending stream of humming, talking and singing that Jamie had kept up since our brush with the logging trucks was getting on my nerves. "Shut up for a while," I said.

It came out louder than I intended and the girl up ahead of us glanced back. It was impossible to know what she was thinking to have come along with us on this wild goose chase in the first place. It was so cold my breath had iced up around my mouth and nose, and every once in a while I'd scrape a mitten across my face to feel the ice crystals shatter. The girl had barely said a word to anyone but her dog, and it seemed to me she'd have been better off back in White Plains.

"Why is she here?" I asked again.

Jamie grinned. "Thought you wanted me to shut up," he said primly.

"Well, first answer my question, then shut up."

Jamie was still grinning an idiotic, loopy sort of grin that gave me the impression he wasn't going to give me a serious answer. If I could have reached him I'd have wiped it off his goofy face.

"She wanted to see the mountains," he said finally.

"Yeah, right. She decided to sit double on a bony mule's ass in freezing cold weather to see a mountain she could see a lot easier from the seat of a nice warm car. Sure."

"No. For serious, man. She wanted to go to the mountains."

I glared at him. "The mountains will still be there in the summer. In a car. On a real road. With a picnic and no snow."

"You don't get it." For once the grin was gone and Jamie was serious. "This is a healing trip for her."

"Yeah, Jamie. Sure. Give me a break."

I was furious with the situation in general, and taking it out on Jamie only seemed natural. I was bored, frozen and hungry and it was still only the first day. Dad was barely talking, Jamie was talking garbage and the Aunts and the girl were sticking to each other like burrs under a saddle. Great trip.

"The mountains are the spiritual home of our people," Jamie said finally and he actually seemed to mean it. He didn't roll his eyes or snort out a laugh. He just kept riding and kept his eyes averted and his mouth shut.

CHAPTER SEVEN

B Y NEXT MORNING our tents were covered in a fresh layer of snow. The zipper of the one Jamie and I shared had frozen shut and inside the tent it was cold but humid from the condensation of our breath.

"I'm not getting up," Jamie moaned from deep in his sleeping bag.

One of the least appealing facets of the trip was this forced togetherness for Jamie and me. Dad had a little A-line for himself, the ladies shared the big dome and Jamie made my life a living hell by sharing the medium dome with me.

He pulled his sleeping bag up over his head and burrowed down until he resembled nothing so much as a huge legless, armless, smooth-skinned larva of some unearthly exotic kind.

"You can't make me. I'll stay here 'til spring," came his muffled voice.

"C'mon." I forced myself to catapult out of the warmth of my bag and pulled an icy flannel shirt on over my long underwear.

"Ooh, what cute little white legs you have," he cooed in a high-pitched voice. "How shapely. How curvaceous. Could no doubt use a shave, but otherwise . . ."

I flicked some of the ice off the encrusted zipper into his face where he peered out of his bag. My jeans from the day before were still frozen solid, but with a dry pair of sweats, two sweatshirts and my hooded parka I felt like a new man sitting there working the zipper while Jamie talked up a storm. He lay at my side, encased head to toe in his bag, extolling the virtues of his little nag.

"Man, she's the nicest little horse," he was saying. "A virtual rhapsody in horse-flesh, the kind of animal any red-blooded Indian would love to have clamped between his manly thighs. Sweet-natured, lovely and calm, but wild and full of energy at the same . . ."

The zipper gave way with a final jerk. I grabbed the foot of Jamie's bag.

"Up," I commanded.

"I think I knew that horse in a former life, she's just so, so . . ." He waved his arms dramatically, searching for the word he wanted, and I yanked hard at his bag.

"Up!" I said again. "Or it's winter wonderland for you, Bud."

". . . So understanding, so sweet, so nice and warm when I myself feel like a giant goosepimple. Hey!"

I heaved hard at the foot of his bag and propelled Jamie through the tent opening into a drift of snow.

"Where am I?" He blinked owlishly at the cold blue cloudless sky and clutched the bag tighter around his neck.

"Mmm," he taunted. "Nice and warm out here. Now I know how all the little mice feel under their blankets of snow. Tiny little tunnels, lots of seeds, teeny little sleeping bags…"

Walking away, I could still hear him carrying on about miniscule earmuffs and little block heaters for the mice's cars. I was disgusted. Jamie's unending company, plus the awful weather, would send me over the edge. I could feel it. Total insanity loomed ever nearer. I pulled another log over to the fire and thumped it clear of snow to use as a seat for breakfast.

"The animals will be there," Aunt Helen was telling Dad as she helped him prop a bucket of snow near the campfire.

They were obviously in the middle of something. Dad's expression was his stubborn one.

"But the place Pete showed me had lots of animals around too, and it's closer."

"We will leave a note. On a tree, in case Pete comes looking for us," Aunt Edith was quietly adamant. "The springs will be warm up there."

"They'll also be sulphurous," Dad mumbled.

"Only near the rocks. Only a smell anyway. Then it's just warm." Aunt Edith tossed a handful of slushy snow into a bowl of flour and began working it around.

The smell of sizzling bacon was so sweet in the cold morning air that first morning. It was almost like you could lick the taste right out of the frosty atmosphere. It was a scent whose memory would come back to tease us later, when we were hungry and our food supplies were low. Aunt Helen carefully poured the excess bacon grease out of the pan and into a little pot she had propped in the snow.

Seeing me watching her, she said quietly, "This will freeze and we can save it. Good for protein when we need it."

Lisa had quietly placed the grill over the fire and popped a frying pan on top. A small dollop of frozen butter began to sizzle its way into a puddle.

"The eggs are frozen." Lisa sounded perplexed.

She looked pretty good in the morning air. Her cheeks were nice and red from the cold, and a little halo of black hair escaped her hat.

"Peel them." Aunt Helen tossed an egg in my direction and one over to Jamie, who'd finally emerged from his cocoon. "Don't be so lazy," she admonished. "No more eggs until the ducks in spring. These are special for today."

Aunt Edith and Lisa were globbing slabs of wet dough onto clean sticks and leaning them over the fire when Jamie and I finished peeling a dozen eggs. I'd never seen bannock made over a fire before. Dad always takes store bread when we camp and Jamie is well-known as a white bread kind of guy. He likes the stuff that gobs up when you take little pieces of it and roll it in your fingers. He likes it for shooting at other people. Or birds or anything else that moves. He's a pretty good shot when it comes to wads of white bread.

"Fry-bread from the fire," Aunt Edith explained, watching me watch Lisa. "Good and hot, and we don't need to wash another frying pan."

Lisa smiled over at me. She had a shy look when her eyes caught mine, but her smile was warm and even.

The golf ball-sized eggs danced and bubbled down into a pool in the frying pan. My mouth was watering. The smell of fresh bannock soaked through the hazy wall of smoke around the fire and, coupled with the effects of Lisa's smile, it made the whole expedition somehow less horribly ridiculous.

"This is great!" Jamie's voice broke the spell and Lisa turned to her dog.

Jamie spread grubby hands in front of the fire and nodded his head for emphasis. "Fresh air! Great food! No school! Where do we go from here?"

"Wolverine Lake," answered Dad, and in unison the Aunts said, "Lynx Creek."

"Okay." Jamie's voice was careful. Even he knew when to leave a subject alone.

"Lynx Creek will be warm. We will leave a note for Pete. If we go higher we will be more comfortable."

Dad's feelings were obviously hurt. He broke off a chunk of bannock and ate in silence, scooping at the yolk of his egg.

I glanced around the circle of faces, uncertain who to back up or what to say, or if I should even say anything at all.

"What's so great about Lynx Creek?" Jamie's mouth was full and his words came out blurred and indistinct with a fine mist of bannock crumbs. Lisa gave him a look of pure revulsion, which somehow made my whole day, and turned her back to toss chunks of warm bannock to the dog, Thor.

"Lynx Creek has warm water. The springs come up from down below and they're hot. We can bathe. Lots of animals at that creek."

"Our old uncle took us there," Edith chimed in.

The two women were like twin elves sitting side by side in matching snowmobile suits with their long braided hair bundled up under rabbit-skin hats. Even the wrinkles in their faces were identical, but they were easy to tell apart. Aunt Edith's eyes were a deep brown, understanding and sorrowful. Helen's were a shocking blue, piercing and questioning.

CHAPTER EIGHT

THE NEXT COUPLE OF DAYS were a blur of mounting, dismounting, saddle sores and frozen fingers. I'd never been so consistently cold in all my life, but that evening over the campfire Aunt Helen gazed long and hard at the moon and pronounced a change coming in the weather.

"You mean it's gonna get colder?" Jamie had been wanting to turn back for the last day and a half.

"That's it then!" He threw his hands in the air. "They'll find our bodies in a couple of centuries and label us Mummy No. 1, Mummy No. 2 . . .," he said, pointing at each of us in turn until Lisa batted his hand down.

"Listen to them, you big jerk," she snapped.

The Aunts, who had been waiting patiently for Jamie to finish, began again.

"There is a ring around the moon," Aunt Edith said. "The weather will change."

Her voice, so quietly sure in the firelight, gave me a shiver.

"The animals are becoming more active," said Aunt Helen.

"They are?" Jamie's disbelief was patently obvious.

She kept on, ignoring the interruption. "There will be change by tomorrow. Or in maybe two days."

"Change for the better, or for the worse?" Dad asked. He held both hands out toward the fire. His fingers were red and chapped after settling the horses in for the night.

Edith shrugged and turned to Helen. Helen looked straight into Dad's eyes and shrugged, too. "Don't know," she said. "Only change."

Jamie dropped his head dramatically into his hands and Lisa nudged him with her elbow. "Have a little respect," she whispered. "They know more than you think they do."

For as long as I can remember, Jamie has treated the Aunts like some kind of joke, and at home we do our best to avoid them. But at the same time, they're great cooks, so hanging at Jamie's means good eating. There's nothing like the Aunts' fry-bread fresh from the pan. And homemade jam. They make saskatoon jam that's like going to heaven.

Jamie laughs at their old-fashioned habits. Makes fun of their clothes and their proclamations. Me, I don't know. I don't make fun of them, that's for sure. There's something in those little wrinkled-apple faces that kinda spooks me. It seems like there's more going on in their heads than just what their mouths are saying and yet, when they're talking about the old days and old beliefs, Jamie puts up such an endless stream of back talk that mostly I end up laughing. Even when I don't think laughing is such a good idea.

Maybe it's wrong to ignore them; maybe we should be taking notes or something, because one of these days they're gonna be gone. Everyone goes down that lonesome trail sometime, and the Aunts are pretty old.

Now Jamie only groaned and looked over at me as Dad got up and left the fire. I watched as Dad's form faded away through the tall trunks of surrounding pines, and then I turned back to the fire.

"She's new," Jamie said to no one in particular, bobbing his head in Lisa's direction. "She's still easily snowed. She needs more experience."

"Jamie, this camping trip is only a small chapter in the long journey of your life," Helen began. "It will be something to tell your grandchildren about. The year you became a man. The time you learned about our mother the earth, from which all of us come and all of us return."

"Oh, yeah." Jamie pushed his chest out and beat feebly on it with mittened fists. "Here I am. Here I stand in the vast wilderness. Man of the Forest. Proud conqueror of all he surveys. The little bunny rabbits bend to my manly will as they hippity-hop through the dark forest glades."

He made the first two fingers of his left hand hop rapidly up Lisa's arm and she knocked his hand away. Aunt Helen snorted, rose and kicked a fallen branch out of her path as she made for her tent. Edith rose, snorted, and kicked at the exact same branch.

After he watched them leave, Jamie grinned over at me and then laughed aloud when Lisa smacked his shoulder.

"Smarten up!" she ordered. "You are the most thankless, infantile jerk I've ever met in my life."

"Ah, thankless! Yes, that's me!" Jamie puffed out his chest and let loose with a Tarzan-style yodel that ended in a fake coughing fit.

"Quit it! You'll scare up a pack of wolves with all that howling."

"Wolves!" He was still playing Tarzan as he turned to face Lisa. "My people think of wolves as cuddly puppies. The wolves are our friends. The wolves suckle our young."

"Oh, brother." I couldn't help thinking he was funny. It must have been a sign of how desperate I'd become for human contact, the fact I'd actually laughed at his ludicrous behaviour, but the look Lisa threw at me stopped me in mid-laugh. Jamie wore an innocently pious expression, which obviously had little effect on her. She flicked a handful of snow in his face.

"Cool off, you drip," she said.

She rose and headed off towards the tent she shared with Thor and the Aunts. She booted the same branch the Aunts had kicked, and sent it flying off into the brush.

"What's with her anyway?" I waited until I was sure she was out of earshot, and even then I found myself whispering.

Something about Lisa and that huge dog Thor made me nervous. The last thing I wanted was for her to somehow overhear me. Instinct told me she wouldn't be too crazy about being a topic of conversation between Jamie and me.

"I still don't understand why she's here in the first place," I complained. "And what's with the guard dog? Who does she think she needs guarding from way out here? Not only that, but doesn't she have to go to school, or work, or something? She's gotta be 18. Where does she live?"

From somewhere behind us Lisa whistled long and low for Thor. He rose from his place near the fire, stretched, bared his teeth in a wide yawn and stalked past me, the hair on the back of his neck rising slightly as he caught my scent.

"Ah, my lovely sort-of-cousin," Jamie began. "You know the Aunts," he prompted. "The crazy women I spend my waking hours with. We're all supposedly related under the skin or something. You remember them. Well, Lisa's even crazier, if that's possible."

Wildly I gestured at him to lower his voice.

"They seem to think every kid they take in is some kind of relative or some-thing," he whispered. "Lisa Buchinski" – he mimicked an old-lady-type voice – "is going to stay with us for a while, sonny. Please introduce her to all your friends and take her to all the little hangouts where you and all your little friends go to play marbles and tell secrets and pick your noses and . . ."

"All right, already." I got the point. "But really, come on, tell me what you know about her."

"Well, she's crazy." He made it sound like the flat-out truth.

"Besides that."

"She's old enough to be your mother, for one thing. And she had some kind of breakdown or something back in the city or someplace."

"Thanks for being so specific." Once again, my javelin thrust of sarcasm was lost on him. "She's not old enough to be my mother, and don't bring my mother into it anyway. My mother's none of your business."

"OK." He held up two hands in surrender. "Point made. But she's actually 19 whole years old. Which is at least old enough to know better. Furthermore, she did have some kind of breakdown. A nervous one, I think."

"You sure?" It seemed a shame, a pretty girl like that.

He nodded solemnly. "Nervous breakdown." He was speaking in a fake-Freud kind of way. "Couldn't take the city life. Too fast-paced. Freaked right out, mein freund. Straightjacket time, Herr Dave."

"What do you mean, 'freaked out'?"

"School. Boyfriend. Who knows?" He shrugged. "It was all too much for her delicate nerves. Just didn't have what it takes, I guess."

"Then you guess wrong!" a cold voice interrupted.

Even Jamie jumped. Lisa was standing directly behind us. She'd heard every word.

"You don't know what my life's been like, Jamie, you liar! You don't know what I've lived through, so shut up." She spoke slowly, with obvious rage in every syllable, but that unusual voice of hers, low and slightly gruff, still made the back of my neck tingle.

"I hated that last place! But Pete and Mike found me and the Aunts let me come stay with them." She sounded near tears. "You will never understand what it was like. After all of it, I had to leave. I had to come back here and find my roots."

"What'd I tell you?" It took more than one enraged female to quash Jamie's natural talent for irritating backtalk. He shook his head, heavy with mock sorrow. "Couldn't take that wild city nightlife."

"You know nothing about me or my feelings. You have no respect for anything." She turned to me, "He doesn't even listen to the Aunts. He laughs at them and he daydreams while they try to talk to him."

"Tsk. Tsk."

Jamie was at it again, jerking her chain, and I was a little surprised she took it all so seriously. He was only kidding around. There's nothing malicious about Jamie; he's just goofy. His hands were clasped under his chin and he assumed what he probably thought was a soulful stare.

"The Aunts," he whispered. "Visionaries. Noble women. Keepers of the one true faith. My heart . . . my heart beats a random tattoo to their words . . ."

"Will you kindly shut the hell up?" There was something beyond anger in her voice now and any hint of tears was gone. "You guys don't know the first thing about me. Quit talking about me."

She turned to leave, then charged back into the circle of light from the fire and shook a forefinger at Jamie. "You don't know how lucky you are, living in that little town with the Aunts and the band council and all the people to look out for you."

"The band council couldn't help my mother," I found myself saying.

She turned to me, then. "You're so lucky. Your dad is just wonderful."

Well, as dads go, he was OK, I couldn't really argue with her there. But to rave about him as 'wonderful' was laying it on a bit thick. Obviously she hadn't had to put up with his infamous silent routine. As I opened my mouth to tell her so, Jamie burst out in an impassioned voice.

"Vunderbar!" he shouted in a fake German accent he'd no doubt picked up from some ancient war movie. "Yah, und also vun heck of an officer . . . intelligent, resourceful, looks good in ze uniform!"

Lisa whacked the back of his head with the flat of her hand. "Smart aleck! Don't make fun of Mike!"

Mike? I was a little surprised, but then at this point nothing much seemed beyond possibility. I couldn't remember Dad ever inviting anyone my age to call him anything but Mr. Beaton, but maybe he was softening out here away from life as we knew it in town. Lisa stormed off to her tent and Jamie leaned over, peering into my face with his nose inches from mine.

"I thought so," he said suddenly. "Don't go getting interested in Cousin Lisa, Dave. She's bad news. And besides, she's old and I think it's illegal."

I bristled. "Who says I'm interested?"

"Well, the drool could give you away." He dodged my fist. "No, seriously, she's antique."

"She doesn't look old. She's actually kind of cute." Especially by firelight, I thought, with those big eyes and her hair all shiny. I'd been pretty impressed with how mad she got at Jamie. Slugging him was something I'd been tempted to do many times.

"And you're kind of desperate. Seriously, leave it alone. I think Thor is actually seeing-eye and she's so old she's going blind as well as being batty."

I let him babble on and tossed a couple more branches onto the dying fire. Lisa had a way of growing on a guy. She wasn't really beautiful, not a model or anything, but she had a way of talking and standing up for herself. I liked her black hair, short and kind of spiky. Her eyes were huge and even more expressive than her voice.

"She has nice eyes," I said.

"Oh, sure, nice eyes!" Jamie was desperate to show me the path of reason as he saw it. "But she's three years older than you, man. And those eyes have seen a lot of guys, if you know what I mean."

"She's got a lot of boyfriends?" The thought didn't surprise me exactly, but the mental image of Lisa's huge dark eyes staring at some other guy gave my gut an edgy sort of feeling.

"Look man." Jamie's voice dropped to a hoarse whisper. "There's stuff you don't know. Maybe you should be talking to your dad."

"So he can tell me the facts of life," I snorted. "Thanks, but I think I can handle that part of it."

"Listen, man," Jamie continued. "I'm serious, now. Don't go after her. Don't ever even try to get close to Lisa or even to understand her. Women are a law unto themselves. I should know; I've lived with two of the weirdest women on the planet since I was three. They're completely off the wall."

Lisa was obviously Aboriginal with a lot of something else thrown in. "I wonder if she came from Edmonton," I mused aloud. "Wonder if she met my mother there."

"Shhh!" Jamie had both forefingers up to his lips. He glanced dramatically over his shoulder at the shadows blanketing the camp. "You dad gets downright psycho, man, every time your mom's name comes up. He's crazy, you know that! No offence."

"Yeah." No offence. I knew what Jamie was talking about. Dad could seem kind of forbidding sometimes.

"Listen, it's all a little sketchy still," he began. "But I've been thinking, man. Thinking of some way of getting our bony selves out of this deathtrap of a camping trip."

He tapped his head vigorously. "Always cogitating. Always ticking over. You might think I've gone to sleep or I'm not paying attention or something, but that's where you're wrong. I'm actually starving for a little action, man, and I think I've got it all worked out . . ."

I interrupted his mumbling. "You know, I bet Pete's the one who found her when he went into the city for Mom's stuff. He had to go sign some papers or something and he was gone for a while. I'll bet he found her on the street or something and maybe she reminded him a little of Mom and so he brought her back out here . . ."

It was my turn to ramble on, but I couldn't get Lisa out of my mind. "That's why Dad acts so strange around her."

"He's not just strange. He's downright . . ."

"OK, OK," I gestured at him to be quiet. "I bet Pete was just helping her out the same way his folks helped my Mom out when she was little."

"I still say keep away from her." Jamie was obviously bored with the conversation. "She's nothing but trouble, and not only that, she's bossy as hell."

He stood and clamped a hand on my shoulder. His voice changed and he assumed a completely fake British accent.

"Well, it's off to the old fart-sack, roomie," he said. "Coming along, old bean-pod?"

Just as I started to say I thought I'd sit up for a little longer, an ear-splitting, unearthly scream ripped through the silent woods behind us.

CHAPTER NINE

"*THE HORSES!*"

Dad stumbled through the flap of his tent, half-dressed, his pants and jacket bundled in his arms. He shivered heavily, partly from the icy blast hitting his long johns, still warm from the sleeping bag, and partly from the fearful scream that lingered in the still night air.

"Dave! The gun!" Hopping awkwardly around on one leg, Dad was trying to pull on his boots at the same time. "The gun!" he hollered again. "Next to my saddle!"

In a daze I fell back over the log we'd been sitting on a moment earlier and reached for the rifle just as another eerie shriek tore through the air.

The shadows of trees ringing the campsite had turned from beautifully mysterious to threateningly gloomy with the onset of the unholy racket. I watched from a kind of fog as Dad, tangled in his pants' legs, kicked out in a furious attempt to get mobile and nearly propelled himself face-first into the fire.

In what seemed like slow motion, I could see myself almost as if from a distance, making a grab at the gun and then, a split-second later, I was dodging down the path towards the area where the horses had been hobbled for the night. The scene had a nightmarish quality that will probably stay with me forever – the deep silence of the forest at night, slashed by wild screams, and the memory of tearing off headlong into unknowable chaos.

It was pitch dark in the woods, the moon's light lending only a fitful glimmer to the branches whipping against my jacket. I could see only the barest outlines of plunging bodies as the horses gave in to their panic and fought against their restraints.

The primeval scream rose in a shivering crescendo that echoed again, ending in a long hissing snarl that made the hairs stand up around my head. I moved forward slowly, concentrating on keeping out of range of the horses' hooves, but close enough to try to find out what was causing the uproar.

It was a scene from an old movie – black and silvery-white, moving shadows and sighing trees, confusion and racketing noise all played out against the ancient silence of the deep forest.

"Cat!" Dad's shout came from somewhere behind me and then I caught Edith's voice, calm in the midst of the melee. "Look at Smoky," she said.

Smoky was a rangy little pinto, known for blowing her sides out when her pack was loaded and then letting the air out when she thought you'd forgotten her, so that her pack hung loose around her belly and slid all over the place. She was as tame as a puppy and just as affectionate, but tonight she was a wild thing, plunging through the snow like a horse possessed.

Perched high on her withers was a huge tawny shape. The mountain lion raked its claws along the side of her neck and Smoky let out a whinny of sheer terror. The hobbles were loosening as she reared, her whinny ending in a half-strangled snort.

"Get him!" Jamie shrieked as he plunged through the woods to one side of me. "Shoot him, man!"

Shoot who? Shoot what? I'd never shot anything but a few empty pop cans. Glancing over my shoulder I could see Dad's jacket somewhere behind me in the trees. The others were back there too, just blurred shapes against the snow.

Smoky was running out of fight. Steam rose in waves from her body as I turned again and pulled the cold heavy rifle up to one shoulder. Everything became silent and nearly still. It was just as well Smoky was tiring since it slowed her down enough for me to take aim. The whole scene was as clear as an etching and moving slow like things seem to do, just at the time you most wish they'd hurry up and be done.

Smoky reared one final time, her front hooves slashing in a helpless way at the air, while the enormous cat on her back hung on, opening its jaws, poised with tremendous grace to stab its fangs at the arched vein in Smoky's neck.

The horse brought her front hooves down and raised her hind end in a vicious twisting buck in a last-ditch attempt at dislodging the cat, and my forefinger squeezed the trigger.

The gun seemed to lower with its own weight while echoes of the shot ricocheted through the surrounding woods, sending the horses into another frenzied spurt of renewed bucking.

"He's dead." Aunt Helen's matter of fact voice broke the spell. "You killed him."

Who's dead? Who killed what? For a second I was dazed with doubt. Had I missed the cat and killed Smoky? She'd said 'he,' so maybe I killed Jamie. I was lost – abandoned in shock. The ice-fogged air filled my head with cold cloud shapes and leant an air of unreality, as if part of me was sitting back as a spectator, only this wasn't a TV show or a video game, it was the real thing.

Dad and Helen were in the midst of the horses, attempting to soothe, to straighten out hobbles and get halters on the heads of the more frantic animals. Speaking softly, patting necks, they moved like spectres through the haze.

Aunt Edith haltered Smoky and led the limping animal over to me. "Here." She handed me the lead and took the rifle from my hands. "Take Smoky to the fire. I need to see the wounds. Build the fire up, make it big. Come on." She prodded a finger at me when I didn't move. "Get going."

She turned to Jamie where he stood right behind me. Good, I thought, I hadn't shot him after all. "Give me a hand," she ordered.

Edith walked off through the mangled snow to where a dark shadow lay on the ground. She grabbed a huge front paw and began to pull. Jamie reached down and took hold of the other paw.

Lisa sat nearby, hugging Thor with both arms around his straining chest to keep him still. His hackles were high, a low growl reverberating nearly soundlessly through his chest. His dark eyes were alert, focused on the dark form, ears pricked forward.

"Better go," Lisa said softly. "Get Smoky to the fire."

The horse nudged my back, her nose warm and questing as I led her away. The trust she showed in me brought a lump to my throat and I could feel tears collecting in a thick mass at the back of my throat. I swallowed hard to keep them back and kept on hiking through the woods to the fire.

"Hey, man!" Jamie bounded into the circle of firelight. "Your Dad said he wants a big fire. They're bringing all the horses closer in case the cat had a mate somewhere. A mate out for revenge. The revenge of a woman, or female kitty in this case, scorned. A woman with a grudge . . ."

"Shut the hell up," I said automatically. I leaned against Smoky, each of us propping the other one up. My stomach was rolling and my knees wouldn't lock properly. By the light of the fire Smoky's gashes were long and sore looking, oozing a dark-coloured blood, which was already beginning to congeal in the frozen air.

"Never knew you could shoot like that, man!" Jamie socked me in the arm. "Just like in the movies. I'm gonna have to call you John. John the man Wayne."

"Did I hit it?" I was still dazed in a state of shock and unsure what was actually happening.

"Hit it! Yeah, you killed him. Point-blank. Boom. Dead."

At least the cat died fast, but the knowledge didn't make me feel any less uneasy and junked up. It gave me something to hold onto, though. And I needed something to hold onto when Dad and Edith gutted the carcass of the cat and hung it from a high branch.

"Bury him," I said.

Edith shook her head. "Mittens." She shoved her hands deep in her pockets and dug out a hankie to wipe her nose. "We'll use the coat for mittens. Maybe a blanket. Thor can have the meat."

My stomach churned as I watched them tie the cat's feet together. He was gorgeous. The fur was a thick tawny gold, the paws huge and soft looking with the nails sheathed, and the fur on his belly was a lighter colour, nearly white in places. He hung there in an unnatural way like some kind of cartoon cat gone awry. His tongue lolled out of his mouth and his tail, a long wiry piece of him that should be tense with life as all cats' tails are, hung slack over his body. His hind feet were lashed to a branch near the trunk of the tree where the wood was thickest.

Helen took a small pouch from around her waist and pinched a bit of dried stuff out, then handed the pouch to Edith. She and Edith took small bits of what looked like dried crumbly leaves and, muttering something, they sprinkled it on the fire.

"Tobacco." Edith spoke in a low voice as she pulled Lisa closer. "We let the energy of the universe take care of us," she explained. "We let our spirits become fresh and whole again. Watch the smoke." A thin line of smoke rose straight up into the air, wavering and then disappearing. "Good for cleaning us after this."

"Good for keeping us together." Helen had her eyes shut and beneath the lids I could see her eyes moving. "Good for keeping us on a straight path."

Staring, unable to calm my guts, I could begin to feel myself lose my supper. I staggered away into the bushes to barf in privacy, too sick to even care if anyone heard me. Behind me I could hear Aunt Edith talking to Smoky while she and Dad examined the horse's neck and shoulders. When I was finished I kicked snow over the mess I'd made and then sat down heavily. I didn't want to have to face anyone back at camp.

Thor sniffed his way over to me. For the first time since we'd met he kept the hair on the back of his neck down. He shmoozled his nose under my hand and sat there with a dopey look on his long face, tongue hanging out. He slid the flat of his head a little more comfortably under my hand and manipulated until he was satisfied. Then he just sat, and so did I.

We sat until I was finally so cold I had no choice but to move. Thor must have been as cold as I was because he followed me back to camp and right up to the flap of Lisa's tent. She was waiting. She opened the flap right away before I even had a chance to whisper her name.

"Thanks for bringing him back." I wasn't sure if she was talking to the dog or me. "Come on, Thor, come on," she coaxed, patting her leg.

Thor left me without a backward glance, crawling into Lisa's tent and lying down with his chin resting on his front paws right next to her sleeping bag.

"Couldn't go to sleep without him," she said quietly.

"He's a nice dog."

Lisa's face was dim and mysterious in the moonlight. With the neck of her parka clutched around her shoulders she was cute and vulnerable looking. She shivered and I wondered if she might invite me in. We could talk. Even with the Aunts sleeping in there we could still talk. I thought it might be good to talk to somebody.

"Well." I began backing away, hoping all the while she'd stop me. "Goodnight. See you tomorrow."

"'Night." The flap of her tent fell shut and she was gone.

My feet were like two blocks of ice as I finally dragged myself across the empty campsite and over to my tent. The cat's carcass hung dimly across the clearing, and with sudden insight I saw myself the way Lisa would – as a barbarian who'd killed an innocent and beautiful animal.

If everything had gone differently, if things hadn't happened so fast, I could have taken a stick from the fire, a torch, and frightened the cat away. A few hours before it had been a wild thing, powerful and tempestuous, and killing it now seemed like the easy way out.

Lisa was smart, of that I was certain. And she loved the outdoors, even Jamie knew that, which meant she'd see me now as a murderer. Hunkering down in my sleeping bag, willing my body to feel warm again, I knew all I wanted in the world was to get my hands on that girl. I wanted to touch her hair, hold her hand, kiss her.

Trouble was, she didn't want me, or my hands or any other part of me anywhere near her.

CHAPTER TEN

PETE ROARED UP on his snowmobile two days later, just as Dad was pouring out the first cup of hot coffee. In the stillness of the woods the noise of the machine growing steadily closer had been audible for at least 10 minutes.

"Supply run!" Pete hollered as he drew up in a swirl of snow.

"You must have a nose for this stuff." Dad was almost smiling as he poured a second cup of coffee.

Even to himself, I don't think Dad was willing to admit how glad he was to see Pete again, but it seemed pretty obvious to me. As far as I was concerned, the sight of someone from outside our little group was just about as good as Christmas morning when I was a kid. The atmosphere in camp had become so tense it felt like a palpable thing. When people talked about cutting the tension with a knife it had always seemed kind of phony to me, but now I thought I knew what they'd been referring to. Shooting the cat had only served to emphasize the distance between Dad and me. He was such an ardent conservationist that I knew he'd probably blame me for the rest of my life for the cat's death. And, for that matter, so would I.

"Did you bring the chinook with you?" Dad handed the coffee to Pete and dusted off a log by the fire. "It's good to see you, Pete."

The Aunts' predictions had proven correct and the weather had indeed changed. A long sighing wind rising high from the west had sounded all through the night, bringing in warmer air over the Rockies from the west coast. By breakfast it was several degrees above the freezing mark. After the last week of numbing cold the change felt as balmy as a summer day.

Even the forest around seemed to be celebrating. The boughs of pine and spruce, which had drooped heavily with snow, released their burdens. Caps of white fell softly, unexpectedly dumping clumps of wet snow onto unsuspecting heads and down necks, then springing upwards again in a kind of dance, showering a mist of icy droplets.

"You know, I'll go just about anywhere for a good cup of coffee," Pete said.

He glanced around the camp circle, eyes stopping flat at the sight of the cat hanging on the far side of the clearing. He let out a low whistle.

"Gonna make some nice warm boot-liners, eh?"

"Mittens," Aunt Helen corrected. "Maybe a hat or two."

Pete nodded and sipped his coffee, his gaze roving the camp area. The place was pretty scruffy, I realized. I watched the flush of embarrassment rise slowly up Dad's face as he suddenly saw the site anew through the eyes of his friend. A collection of cooking utensils and pots lay discarded in a haphazard pile at one side of the fire, while a pot of soapy water slowly cooled at the other. The hatchet lay beside one tent, where it had been dropped earlier after being used to trim branches for kindling, and a million bits and pieces of junk needed for camping were scattered around like bits of confetti after a particularly messy wedding.

Although the rest of the horses had been tethered behind the camp up against the wall of bush, I saw Pete's eyes come to rest on Smoky with her torn-up neck and shoulders. The Aunts and Dad had decided to give her an extra day's rest before expecting her to join us on the trail, but if anything, the little horse looked worse today than she had the morning after her tussle with the mountain lion. Her head drooped slightly and she looked as if her legs could barely hold her up. I felt a sudden surge of resentment that Pete would take one quick look around and then jump to conclusions about the events we'd faced out here in the woods.

"Pretty bad, isn't it?" Dad said quietly. His tone was combative. "Don't start making me take notes on winter survival now, Pete."

Pete took a long sip of coffee. "Looks like you can use a few supplies," was all he said.

"Don't need them." I had half-expected Dad's belligerence, but I saw Lisa throw him a surprised look. He hates being judged by anyone, but especially by Pete. "We can trap for meat."

There was a tense silence broken by Helen's calm voice. "Rations are getting low," she said. "Might have to eat the cat."

I could feel my face redden with revulsion and saw Dad's own mix of disgust at the idea of eating the cat combine with an anger he was obviously struggling to control.

"Or trap squirrel, snare a rabbit," put in Edith.

"Squirrel," Lisa stated firmly. "I don't think any of us want to eat the cat, but maybe Thor won't be so picky."

She glanced fondly at her dog as she spoke and I felt a sudden warmth pour through me. It was nice, that relationship she had with the animal. She was OK. Even after all she must have seen, all she must have gone through to make her leave the city and find a haven out in the boonies with the Aunts. Even then, she still had that softness inside her for her dog.

"Who killed him?" Pete asked, gazing directly at the cat's carcass.

"Me." The sound of my voice surprised me. Even to my own ears it sounded strained and a little shaky.

"Didn't mean to," I found myself mumbling. "It just happened."

"Luckily for Smoky," Lisa said.

"Yeah, lucky for Smoky," Pete agreed, nodding in the horse's direction. "You don't have a hunting licence?"

"No."

"Were you in bodily harm?"

"No."

"Big cats have a very restricted hunting season."

"You gonna arrest him?" Jamie was all enthusiasm. "Throw him in the slammer, maybe?"

Once again I couldn't help wondering what on earth had possessed Dad to allow Jamie on the trip. At the time it had seemed a decision that could have used a little more thought, but now the constant companionship was nearly driving me around the bend. He had become a major pain.

"Of course, you're part Indian, some parts of you anyway," Pete continued, ignoring Jamie's interruption. His voice was quiet, ruminative. "Part something else, too. You're out here on your own. It isn't as though you're a bunch of thieving cowardly trophy hunters."

"I wish it never happened," I said and I meant it.

Pete tossed his coffee grounds into the fire. "I know," he said.

Edith had been silently ladling porridge into tin bowls. "That cat was hungry," she declared. "It wouldn't have gone after a big animal like a horse otherwise. Cats are smart. He saw the hobbles and thought dinner was ready."

"So close to a fire and people," Helen chimed in. "He knew we were here, but he must have gambled on less fight than Smoky had in her."

"Maybe the cat was sick." Edith blew on a spoonful of oatmeal.

"But probably just hungry." Helen began eating.

"Didn't look sick." Edith was obviously enjoying her breakfast. She spooned more sugar into her bowl and stirred it through the oatmeal. "Hide is nice and soft," she continued. "Good colour, full. Eyes are clear. Just hungry, that one."

"Probably the hunting was hard," Lisa broke in. "The snow's so deep, right? The snow is deep, the temperature's been way down below normal for weeks . . ."

Dad was smiling at her as she spoke. She sounded like a little kid trying to impress a teacher. And then I banished the thought. Why would she be trying to impress anyone, Dad least of all? He'd done absolutely nothing to encourage any of us to speak to him for days. In fact, it seemed to me he'd bent over backwards to ignore everyone even more than normal since the night the cat appeared. He tossed his oatmeal onto the fire, and got up to go to the horses.

"They're way under the snow, right?" Lisa asked. "Those little mice are only a mouthful. All that digging for a bite of fur and bones. He was so hungry. He needed food and the horses were standing there hobbled and sleepy. I bet the cat's only problem was he was too young to know better."

"You've thought it all through." Pete grinned.

"Aunt Edith says all living things have a soul," Lisa replied. "The earth, trees, animals, even rocks; they're all tied in together. They balance each other. We are the ones who upset the balance."

"Good," Helen said approvingly. "Too bad others don't listen and learn the way you do. The wild places are a good place for people to learn about life's cycles."

"Learn about themselves, too," Edith put in and glanced around the circle at each of us in turn.

"Some need these things more than others," Helen added.

The last remark seemed aimed at Jamie. He rolled his eyes and made a face. "Cockamamie," he said.

"I beg your pardon?" Lisa was insulted.

"Froot Loops," Jamie announced. "Squirrel bait, nutzoid . . ."

"Shut up!" The sound of my own voice surprised even me.

I'd been purposely keeping the lowest profile possible, but Jamie's voice seemed to have finally breached the limits. None of these people were people I wanted to be around anymore, except possibly for Lisa. The Aunts with all their talk of trapping animals for food and skinning cats for mitts were just too gruesome to be believed. Then there was Dad, who hadn't talked to me at all for days on end, at least not about anything important, and who didn't seem to deserve my attempts to talk to him anymore. Finally there was Jamie, who just never seemed to close his mouth for a second.

"You're driving me nuts, man!" To my own surprise, I was yelling. "You never stop talking. You talk all the time; even at night in your sleep you talk. It's driving me crazy! Just shut up for a while, will ya?"

Thor shoved a wet nose under my palm and worked his head through until my hand rested on the flat of his forehead. Thor, Dog Psychologist.

"Can we move on to another topic of conversation besides dead cats?" My voice sounded a little high, even to my own ears, and I fought to lower it. "Anything else, believe me. Anything."

The rest of the group was silent as I scanned their faces. "I couldn't help killing him," I said finally. "I could barely even see. It was a lucky shot. If you want to know the truth, I am not a great hunter and I hated doing it. I just didn't know what else to do."

I managed to stop myself just short of whimpering like a little kid that all I really wanted to do was go home again.

CHAPTER ELEVEN

I N THE QUIET THAT FOLLOWED my outburst we finished off the oatmeal, tossing our empty bowls into the pot of hot snow water for rinsing.

"Surprised to find us still alive?" Dad's voice was restrained, but it sounded almost combative as he spoke to Pete. I could sense the tension behind the words. For some reason, he was filled with anger. One by one the others got up from their places and began the work of breaking camp.

"It's only been a week," Pete reasoned. "I was hoping you hadn't resorted to cannibalism yet."

"We might decide to boil Jamie up one day." Lisa's voice was dreamy. She rolled her sleeping bag into a tight ball and gave it a solid punch.

"He only talks. He's harmless." Dad seemed bent on reassuring her, which surprised me a little since he doesn't normally seem to care one way or another how people are feeling. He doesn't joke around like Pete or try very hard to make friends.

"He's probably learning about rocks' souls by osmosis." Pete grinned. "One day it'll all come pouring out and he'll be a great spiritual guru for all us old heathens."

Dad gave a short laugh, but Aunt Helen was all seriousness.

"It's in his blood," she began. "The great uncle of his mother, Frank Black Coyote, was a shaman. He was both feared and respected by the old ones. He spoke with the souls of those who went before."

"How did he do that?"

The interest in Dad's voice amazed me and I saw Pete shoot him an odd look.

"He practised the sweetgrass ceremony. He used the sweat lodge. He was from the old ways."

"I'd like to know more about this uncle," Dad said. "Might make a good painting," he added lamely.

Jamie glared across the campfire at Dad. It was obvious he'd heard enough about this famous uncle of his to last him a lifetime.

"You'll be too busy to be hanging around in sweat lodges," Pete said. He reached into an inner pocket and pulled out a handful of envelopes. "Here." He held the mail out to Dad.

"We've left all that behind." Dad spoke quietly. "Nobody asked you to play mailman, Pete. Take it all back where it came from."

"Could be a nice fat commission. Maybe a cheque or two." Pete waved the envelopes in the air in a tantalizing way.

"Money is only paper out here. It's worthless."

"Come on, it might be important." Pete tossed the envelopes down on a clear spot near the fire. "Only five letters, no junk mail."

Standing suddenly, Dad splashed the remains of the dishwater over the fire. He kicked snow through the embers, his movements emphasizing each word. "Take it back, Pete. We're on our own out here. We don't want any of your outside-world help."

"You want the supplies, though." Pete was like a dog with a bone, endlessly worrying it. "I figured you guys might be ready for a fried egg or two, maybe a steak."

The Aunts had stopped packing up and were silently watching Dad.

"No supplies," he said. "Don't need them."

"Never coming back, huh? Planning on living off the land indefinitely? You might need those when you come back to civilization." Pete gestured at the letters still lying where he'd dropped them. His voice had a hard edge that rivaled Dad's.

Dad stood for a long silent moment, his hands at his sides, and then looked again at Pete. "We won't be back."

The Aunts exchanged a look, and I thought, a little giddily, that maybe we better start trapping a few things after all.

Jamie glanced from face to face in an uneasy way. He leaned over and whispered at me while Dad's and Pete's voices rose in the background.

"Hey, Dave, aren't we ever going back? We're staying out here forever? I kinda thought of it as a little vacation from school, that's all."

The worry on his face, pushed so close to mine, was almost comic, and I couldn't resist jerking his chain a little. Revenge, I figured, for all the endless yakking he'd been doing.

"I don't know," I said slowly, as if weighing each word. "We might go back, someday. Some year. Just for a visit.

"On the other hand, who knows? We might all die out here. In our old age, of course. Still melting snow down for tea, still rationing the oatmeal, still half-frozen all night in our mangy old sleeping bags."

Jamie glanced again at Dad and Pete, who had now lapsed into an uneasy silence.

"What about the powwow next summer?" His voice rose to an outraged whine. "I was gonna be there. I had big plans, man!"

"I thought you didn't believe in the old Indian ways," Pete said. "Thought you didn't have any use for teepees, peace pipes, eagle feathers and all the rest."

"I don't, but you should see the chicks at these things!" Jamie mopped his brow theatrically. "Beautiful, man! I figured I could maybe get a job selling Coke or something and meet some girls. They must get awful thirsty after all that dancing."

"Coke!" It was Lisa's voice, coming from the travois she was helping Edith repack. "Coke! That figures!"

"Wha-a-a-t?" Jamie uttered the word as a long-drawn whine.

"It figures you would go to a powwow and sell a white man's drink. It figures as soon as you mention a beautiful tradition, passed down from the ancestors, it's only to make some filthy money off it. Coke! You should be learning to drum, or something. You should be dancing and honouring your ancestors."

"Honour, shmonour." Jamie got up and started towards the horses. "I can't do anything right around here," he shot back over his shoulder. "You're all so doggone 'honourable' – you're like some kind of walking, talking totem poles."

"Saddle up!" Dad had been busy, loading animals with the help of the Aunts. "We're here for good or bad, Jamie. Go back with Pete if you don't like it."

"He doesn't mean it, Jamie." I grabbed the letters up and shoved them into the back pocket of my jeans. Dad can be pretty harsh sometimes. "Come on," I insisted, surprising even me. "You're part of the team now; you've got to come with us."

We were kind of a rabid, unruly team, all pulling in different directions, but still a team, I thought. I couldn't see Dad's eyes, but the Aunts exchanged a solid look, and for a split-second I even felt kind of good about the trip again, as if maybe it would eventually prove to be not such a bad idea after all.

"Time to saddle up," Aunt Edith told Jamie in one of those tones that make you realize how much you value your life. "Pete, it was good to see you." She turned to Lisa. "Time to go. Come on, girl."

From high up on her mule, Edith held out her left foot. Lisa used it to hoist herself onto the animal's rump, whistling for Thor as she rose.

Pete grinned over at me and shook his head. He was never a man to hold a grudge. "Where you off to?" he called to Dad's stiffened back.

"Lynx Creek," I answered when it became clear Dad wasn't going to.

Ajax's reins were tightly looped in my left hand. I hoped for once in his life he'd hold still long enough for me to shinny on up without completely embarrassing myself. Ajax turned his long sad face and nibbled at my leg, waited until he felt the pressure of my arms on his back in preparation for mounting, and then hopped his hind end around just far enough for me to lose my grip. Typical. I'd been riding bareback since the first afternoon because I liked the warmth, but climbing aboard was always a battle of wills.

"Hey, boy." I crooned a senseless little refrain, hoping to distract him. "It has warm water," I said by way of explanation to Pete. "Lynx Creek, I mean."

Holding tight to the reins, I followed Ajax around in a narrow circle. It had become a daily dance for the two of us; it seemed to amuse him, and it made us nearly always the last ones ready for the trail.

The only thing that seemed to get Ajax's attention was for Dad and the others to start heading out and then, since he seemed to be terrified of being left behind without his buddies, he'd usually sidle coyly back in my direction and hold still long enough for me to pull myself up.

"Lynx Creek is a hot spring," Helen called back to Pete.

"It's a holy place," Lisa added, somewhat unnecessarily I thought, since any mention of the word 'holy' seemed like an invitation to a private snark party where Jamie was concerned.

"Must be interesting," Pete mused, "on the road with all these diverse-type people."

"Yessir," Jamie tossed back. "One endless chuckle, let me tell you." He cocked a forefinger at Dad, who was working at getting his ponies untangled and whose mood was not improving with the exercise.

"The boss is one hilarious guy," Jamie said. "And of course Cousin Lisa is nothing if not an endless font of unwanted useless information."

Lisa stuck out her tongue and Pete laughed. "Maybe I'll make another trip out in a couple of weeks. See if any of you are still on speaking terms."

Dad heaved a sigh that could be heard even above the creaking of saddles as he turned back. "Sorry, Pete."

"OK." The chinook breeze tossed Pete's coat flaps, gusting warmly through the clearing. The wind's caress made me glad to be alive, glad to be on the move.

Dad pulled his hat down tighter and clicked his tongue at Stanley. "Got to set up a permanent camp," he muttered back at Pete, "or we'd stay and talk longer."

"Sure. I know. Good luck, partner."

Dad nodded, snapped a salute at Pete, and began leading his pack string slowly out of the clearing and up onto a low rocky outcrop. The horses stumbled and snorted, giving their usual signs of annoyance at being forced to work again. Smoky was at the tail end, packed lightly, tossing little annoyed bucks and snapping at the horse in front as her hooves clattered over rock and ice.

Helen hoisted Pete's sack of food over the horn of her saddle. "This will be good," she said. "Thank you."

"See ya, Pete!" I called out when Ajax finally stood still long enough for me to wedge the upper part of my body over his back. He was off, following the others, before I could pull myself upright.

A few seconds later, Pete was hidden by intervening trees as we reined the horses onto a narrow deer trail, heading deeper into the fold of mountains.

It felt good to be moving again. Even one extra night in a place felt too long now. I experienced a sudden warm surge of affection towards Ajax, my dauntless steed as I sometimes thought of him. We were a team, a combat team, trusting each other, watching out for the other guy. Facing down the enemy side by side, or one on top and one below in our case, out there in the line of fire, leading the squad over the top. It was downright inspiring.

Making an unexpected hop to one side, Ajax did his best to scrape my leg off on a nearly poplar.

Of course, there was always the question of whether the other member of our little combat team felt the same way about me. I doubted it. Every day was like this, full of little stops and starts, bucks and low-hanging tree branches, a horse's version of rider-torture, played out to the whims of my fearless beast.

"Ride 'em, cowboy," Lisa murmured with a wicked laugh as she passed on Edith's mule.

The sight of Lisa riding in front of me put all other concerns out of my mind. She made a pretty picture, sitting straight and tall on the rump of the white mule, her jacket swinging open and the sun shining her hair to a silver-black cap. She bounced a little to the animal's motion, her dog trotting faithfully alongside.

Thor's tongue hung out one side of his mouth and he cast furtive, slavishly affectionate glances at her now and then – the same look I could sometimes feel on my own face.

"Man, you gotta do something about the sappy look on your mug." Jamie had drawn even with me. "Don't tell me you've got the hots for my little old almost-a-cousin. You are just too weird, man."

He peered into my face, his expression openly curious. I snapped back, exasperated. "Shut up," I barked. "Keep your stupid voice down."

"Oh, no, I knew it," he moaned. "I knew you were getting all mushy over her. Don't do it! Fight it! She's a nut, that girl. Just listen to all that crap she gives the Aunts. She's got all kinds of crazy ideas, and besides she's old, really old and off-limits. Off, man, off." He whistled a short tune and slapped the reins against his leg. "And anyway, the Aunts would be pissed. Really mad at you. We'll find you a hot chick next summer at the powwow. One for you and one for me."

I kicked Ajax into a reluctant trot, which, because of the pain involved, I normally tried to avoid. His withers were like a blade in my crotch. At this rate, I'd be lucky to be able to maintain any kind of romantic interest in anything.

Pulling ahead of Jamie, I could hear him call out, "And it's illegal! I told you, it's probably illegal!" I groaned aloud as his voice rose. "Everything fun is against the law," he hollered. "You oughta know that. And the Aunts'd kill you. But first they'd make you suffer, man. Remember those war movies? Remember Clint Eastwood making people pay the price?"

He laughed and coughed a little. "Man, the Aunts taught Clint Eastwood everything he knows about being a tough guy. He was a scrawny wuss when he met them. And they are watching out for our friend Lisa."

I was furiously angry. That guy had better learn to clam up once in a while, I fumed under my breath. His babbling about Lisa being crazy and things being illegal and all was not only insulting the girl I thought I might be falling in love with, but it was also monotonous. I was almost 16, I reminded myself, old enough to know what I wanted. Old enough to be making my own choices. Almost voting age, and therefore legal age to be falling for Lisa. Legal in my own mind, at least. Just like with every topic Jamie started holding forth about, 90 per cent of what he had to say was nonsense – empty words filling empty air.

Flipping the end of a rein idly against Ajax's neck, I vowed I'd never speak to the jerk again if Lisa had caught even one syllable of his stupid remarks. I had every intention of telling her I was crazy about her, or not telling her, all in my own good time, and I didn't need help from Jamie or anyone else.

CHAPTER TWELVE

THE CHINOOK ARCH LASTED the better part of two weeks, and when the cold finally did descend again it hardly mattered anymore. Things were finally settling into a sort of predictable rhythm. Of course, hardly anyone was speaking to anyone else unless absolutely necessary, but for a man like Dad who valued silence above all else this was not a hardship.

In my own case, things were different. I happen to like talking. It's a necessity for me, and at home there's always somebody, even the odd teacher, to shoot the breeze with. I'm not good at keeping stuff inside; it seems to just boil up and demand to be let out like a kettle whistling on the stove. Under normal circumstances I can usually rely on Pete's visits for a bit of a break, if Dad's in one of his moods and there aren't any friends handy.

Conversations with Dad are limited even at the best of times, but now they were confined to absolute necessities as he drew further and further into himself. Spilling anything to the Aunts was something I never had been really comfortable with, since in some weird way it felt like confiding in either of them was somehow disloyal to Jamie, whose firm opinion on the Aunts was well-known. At the same time, I could see them watching me sometimes, particularly when Lisa was in the vicinity and I wished there was a stronger tie so that maybe I could confide in an Aunt and get her view on things. The only one doing any steady talking out here was Jamie, whose contribution to the general aura in camp was basically a smoke-screen of utter crap.

On the plus side, the hot spring itself was everything the old sisters had promised. Breaking through at the edge of a nameless lake, it brought warm, slightly sulphurous water from some source deep within the earth's core. Warmed by the benevolent hot spring, tiny wild flowers bloomed nearly year-round, pushing their way up through any minute crack in the granite where they could gain a foothold.

Day to day concerns with preparing meals and keeping warm had brought life down to a basic level, which, in theory at least, was supposed to heal Dad's wounds. All I knew was that we were finally setting up a more permanent camp and maybe now the work of healing and finding peace and strength could finally get started, since the sooner Dad felt he'd resolved his issues, the sooner we could head back home again. All I really wanted anymore was to be able to go into my own room and close the door.

But before any of that could happen we needed a more permanent shelter than the tents could afford. And by the time the Aunts got through drawing up floor plans in the snow, selecting the straightest saplings, pointing out the spongiest pine boughs and generally bossing everybody around, we found to our own surprise we'd actually constructed a rudimentary lodge of sorts.

It seemed a little overdone to me. After all, the weather was fantastic – warm and sweet with a hint of spring already in the air. Winter seemed to have run its course, the way it can sometimes in the foothills when spring comes extra early. The two old Aunts, though, had insisted we protect ourselves from the elements, and once I got a second to stand back and take a look at the structure I had to admit we'd done a pretty good job.

The place wasn't very big, but it was large enough for all of us to sleep in with a little privacy provided by hanging a tarp. The Aunts had insisted on a single dwelling because they thought the combined body heat would help all of us stay warmer at night. Not that I was complaining, since any break from being stuck alone with Jamie seemed like progress to me.

The saplings we'd cut on that first afternoon provided support, braced as they were with the tops leaning inward, their bottom ends jammed as securely into hard-packed snow as possible. They were roped together and counterbalanced by guy ropes attached to the lower trunks of surrounding pine and poplar. Long pine boughs lashed to the saplings provided the roof and sides of a long, squarish teepee. We provided extra weather protection by spreading the tents and their fly-covers out flat over the roof, sealing our home as well as we could. There was no doubt in my mind the place would be impossibly damp and leaky during the spring melt.

At night our sleeping bags were spread over a floor of pine boughs covered by a tarp, which we rolled up religiously every morning. It was an Aunt rule – make your bed, or face the consequences. Nobody so far had cared enough to defy them and find out what the consequences might be. Every couple of days, whenever the mood would strike, one or the other of the Aunts would insist on a general airing out of our little abode, and all the bags had to be brought outside and draped over tree branches inside-out, while some unlucky sod used a branch to sweep snow and various outdoor debris off our tarp floor.

I had to admit, though, the lodge was snug and warmer than the dome tent had been. The tarp, which had been hung to provide privacy, divided the place into boy and girl sections. It was great. Sometimes. Other times it got a little too close for comfort.

Lisa was nothing if not modest. She did all her dressing on the girl side behind the tarp, she only went to visit the hot pool with the Aunts and Thor as chaperones and she was careful not to surprise or be surprised in any moments of undress. She was driving me crazy with desire.

Jamie, on the other hand, was simply driving me crazy. His endless talk actually forced me to develop a stronger appreciation for Dad's equally endless silences. Dad would have been happier if none of us had been there. He went out of his way not to speak to anyone, least of all me. He talked to the Aunts once in a while, when the business of running the camp made it absolutely necessary, and he'd developed some kind of friendship with Lisa, which, I am embarrassed to admit, nearly made me foam at the mouth with jealousy. Towards me, Dad had been mostly silent. He would have made a great monk in some remote monastery.

Anything was preferable, though, to Jamie's non-stop, marathon ruminations on life, love and the girls at next summer's powwow. The man's mouth was like an unstoppable force of nature.

And then there was laundry day. The toughest day of all. The sight of Lisa's stuff draped over the lower branches of a poplar we'd dubbed 'the hanging tree', lying only an intimate branch or two from my own, had a strange effect on my nervous system. It seemed to drive all reasonable thought from my mind, leaving only a gluey rumble of dark, delightful torment.

Jamie seemed to have thought that once out on the trail he'd never have to wash himself or anything else ever again, and in that he was disappointed. The spring itself was small, only big enough to submerge a single person at a time, but at the same time it was enough to keep ourselves and some of our clothing reasonably clean, even if we did all smell a little of sulphur. Once the hot water from the spring hit the lake edge it diluted with the colder water and froze almost immediately, but before that it provided enough warmth for tiny plants to flourish. Near the centre of the small whirlpool the water was sometimes so hot it hurt, and on other days it was only lukewarm throughout, giving us a small sense of what was going on under the earth's crust.

"Dave!" Dad barked as I returned to camp one day and dumped a batch of clean underclothes on a sleeping bag to be sorted. "Give the Aunts a hand with the snares, will you? Then go out and bring in some more kindling."

And good afternoon to you too, I thought. Aloud I said, half-angrily, "You're turning into a real sergeant major, you know that? You ought to be leading a bunch of tormented legionnaires through the Sahara or something."

"Just do what you're told." Dad's sense of humour was in real short supply these days, but I was now on a roll.

"The Foreign Legion doesn't know what it's missing in you," I continued. "You know what you need? You need to open those letters Pete brought and start drawing again."

As soon as the words were out of my mouth I was wishing them back. The wrong tactic with Dad is any tactic different from the one he's using himself. He doesn't take well to sarcasm or even another opinion when he's in one of his moods, and he'd been in one of his moods ever since they found Mom's body.

And that's another thing: I sometimes felt I really needed to unload on somebody, explain my feelings, talk about what happened to her, but out here there was no one I could turn to. I sometimes thought the Aunts would be willing to listen if I gave them a chance, but they were always busy patching stuff up or cooking up a meal or skinning some little animal, and I just never found the opportunity. It's not easy changing long-term habits, and the habit between me and the Aunts was for me to keep to myself. There were times I wished this could be different.

"When I want your opinion, I'll ask for it," Dad snarled. He was as mad at me as he had been with Pete several days earlier. "You're only a kid, Kid, so get going. You don't know what I need."

Maybe not, but I knew what I needed and it sure wasn't this. Resentment toward him, his silence, his demands, his rules and him in general made a sour taste in my mouth, but since I still valued what life I had, I knew better than to mention it. "Sorry," I muttered, not meaning it.

He glared at me for a second longer before all the air seemed to go out of him and he sagged down at the shoulders. Pulling a log closer, he sat down heavily and motioned me to join him.

"I know these past weeks have been hard on you," he began slowly. He rubbed a thoughtful hand over the stubble on his chin and examined his fingernails for a couple of minutes before continuing. "It's been hard for me, too."

His voice was so quiet I could barely hear him, and yet I was afraid to break the spell by speaking. Leaning forward, I picked up a little stick and began peeling it as a way of keeping my fingers busy and my eyes focused somewhere other than on him.

"Losing your Mom that way and coming out here," he started. "The Aunts say I need to talk to you and they're right. I know they're right, but it's not easy, not what I have to say." He stopped again and his eyes wandered around the camp area as if searching for a way out.

"You know," he continued, finally, "there are things we haven't talked about yet, Dave. There's probably lots of time," he said reassuringly, as if that thought might give him a way out of the conversation, "but still, maybe we should start hashing some stuff over. I'm not good at talking about these things, but you've probably got some questions you'd like to ask."

He stopped for a minute and looked out over the camp. "There'd be other people better at answering them for you, though and maybe dragging you out here wasn't such a good idea after all."

"No, Dad, it was a great idea. Honest." Seeing him so uncertain was a little scary. It didn't seem right, and I wanted to build him up again. "The best idea you've had in a long time."

"Even with Jamie for company?" Dad had split up a near-fistfight between the two of us the day before over Jamie's sloppy bathroom habits.

"Yean, even with Jamie."

Dad gave a short laugh. A link seemed to form between us, if only a thin thread, a strand. We hadn't had anything like this in weeks and I suddenly realized how much I'd missed it.

He cleared his throat, serious again. "Look, Dave, we've got to talk about something and it's not going to be easy."

"Better save the talk. Lots of time for talk when it's cold again." Edith had come up unheard and now stood directly behind us. "Going to be a change in the weather," she said.

The interruption was maddening. It was a beautiful afternoon, the kind of winter afternoon that makes you wonder why everyone makes such a big deal about summer. The sun was bright, the air warm with a clean sharp smell to it, the slight breeze was as soft as a blanket and the snow was bright white.

Sure, the sun still sank behind the mountains awful early each day, but we all knew that in a few weeks we'd begin seeing the pendulum swing the other way and the days would be noticeably longer. It seemed only a waiting game now until the really warm weather began.

"Aw, come on, Aunt Edith." I didn't want to break the rhythm I had going with Dad. "It's a terrific day. Quit worrying."

Helen joined us. She had the kindest smile; it broke her face in a crooked vee. "It's a long way to spring, yet," she said. "The clouds are changing colour. Sun dogs right there." She pointed at a couple of little rainbow things vaguely visible on either side of the sun. "Wind's moving around a little. Going to be from the northeast by tonight. Watch the sky, David. Smell the air and you will smell snow, lots of it, on the way."

At her words Dad got to his feet and became all business again. "Dave, get that kindling. Pile it as high as you can before dark and I'll find Jamie. We'll need to make sure the horses are comfortable and safe."

"Dad! Slow down! It's a great day; let's just enjoy the weather and you can tell me the stuff you wanted to talk about."

Edith looked narrowly at Dad. "You haven't talked to him?"

"Not now," Helen said. "Later."

"Find Lisa, too, Dave!" Dad barked. "She's out checking snares with Thor. Bring them both into camp and don't forget the kindling!" he hollered after me.

CHAPTER THIRTEEN

"DON'T FORGET," I MIMICKED. "Get Lisa and don't forget!"

He made it sound like I was about five years old and not only that, but five years old with problematic short-term memory loss.

A few days earlier, Edith had taken an old frayed tarp and cut it up into carry-alls. I slung a couple of them over my shoulder for holding the kindling before stomping my way out of the clearing. Taking the deer trail we used as our main highway out of town, I made sure I got out of there fast.

Scaremongers. I was as angry with the Aunts as I was with Dad. I was totally sick of being interrupted, being out of the loop – some fifth wheel on the edge of things, who nobody seemed to ever include in their lives. When Dad tells a person he's got something to talk to them about it's nearly always something he's been stewing over for ages and it's nearly always something a guy actually would like to know about since that's the reason Dad's been stewing about it in the first place. Obviously.

Paranoids. The sooner I got out of this friggin' place the better. I'd never really thought much about leaving home before, since the time always seemed so far away, but the events of the last few weeks made me wish for the day I'd be 18 and officially an adult. I'd be gone. As far gone as I could get. I figured I'd be better off on my own anyway, since the zero privacy and constant companionship of the weirdos on this trip was making me nuts. Once again I found myself wishing I'd never laid eyes on any of them. Escape seemed the only way out. But escape to where? We were miles away from anything out here and there was really no place to go.

The thought of getting away from all of them just wouldn't leave me. It hung in the back of my mind like a dark curtain hiding something I needed to see. Run away and find a new set of problems, I told myself. Answer only to me. Make my own decisions. New problems, no matter what they were, would be better than all this tiptoeing around Dad, worrying about hurting his feelings, scared he'd turn himself so far away from me I'd never find him again.

Thunderstorms from years back had left a lot of deadfall farther east, and automatically I made my way in that direction. Dry wood was plentiful there and would be easy to gather up.

Coming across Lisa and Thor's trail as I walked was an unexpected bonus. Now I wouldn't need to turn the joint upside down searching for them. In my current state of mind anything requiring actual brainpower or the least physical exertion didn't sound too appealing. I intended to do only the minimum required and then crawl into my sleeping bag and turn my back on the world.

At any rate, tracking Lisa had a lot more appeal than fetching sticks. Standing there, where her trail crossed the one I was following, I shrugged. Who was I to turn down a gift like this? The wood could wait; I'd find Lisa first. That thought seemed to brighten the afternoon, especially when I easily caught up to her in a thicket of brush about a mile uphill, resetting a snare under a bunch of willows.

"Something's been in here," she called out when Thor's bark alerted her to my presence. "Whatever it was, it got out again, but I don't think it could have been very big or the trap would have held. I wish Edith were here to tell me what kind of tracks these are."

She was crouched in the snow, behind a screen of little willow branches, studying the messed-up, tracked-up snow around her as if she were Sherlock Holmes hot on a case. Just call me Dr. Watson, I said to myself, and hunkered down, pushing the twigs aside, to crawl into the thicket next to her.

"Looks like Thor kind of messed up the tracks himself," I offered. Down on the ground beside her I glanced at the turmoil of dog, girl and beast tracks around the snare. "I don't think Edith could sort this mess out."

Lisa laughed, giving me a quick glimpse of white teeth and dancing eyes under straight brows. "You'd be surprised what Edith can figure out from a few hairs or a broken branch."

Or at least, I thought, what Edith wants us to believe she's figured out. Aloud I said only, "Yeah, Edith's a wonder, all right."

It seemed the only thing I could say that would keep her there beside me. Both Aunts' talents were actually lost on me most of the time; I tended more to resent their interference in my life. Helen's eyes seemed to go right through a guy, and I sensed she guessed what my real feelings for Lisa were and that she wasn't terribly thrilled about it. Even now, just thinking about those sharp little blue eyes being turned in my direction made a chill run down my spine.

"It's interesting, you know." Lisa stretched out a hand, parting the willow branches where they curved over us. She stood then and stretched as I pulled myself up beside her. "Edith once tracked a rabbit from our snare and found where its burrow was. The trail was all over the place, just like this mess here, and she sorted it all out. She's amazing."

"Yeah. Amazing."

Standing there, Lisa and I were almost the same height. I like tall women. Her face was only inches from mine. I leaned a little forward, and to my surprise she didn't back away. She stood her ground.

"What's going on, Dave?" Her voice was quiet, level, nearly a whisper.

Our lips were almost touching and I felt vaguely encouraged by the fact that so far she hadn't screamed and run away. She was looking straight into my eyes, with the most honest expression I'd ever seen, straight into my soul.

I moved in just a fraction more and our lips touched, only lightly, before she sprang back a step or two.

"Dave, listen," she began.

"Shhh." I didn't want anything to ruin the moment. I knew what she was going to say anyway – that I was too young or too immature or something. For a moment we only looked at each other, and then I reached out a hand and slowly stroked her hair. She leaned her head lightly into my palm like an animal being petted.

"C'mon." My voice was hoarse.

"Dave." Her voice held a warning.

"C'mon, I know you want to," I whispered back. I was being as seductive as I knew how. Dropping my voice to the barest whisper so she had to lean slightly toward me to hear, I said, "Come on, Lisa. Just a kiss."

The hand not stroking her hair reached out and felt for her hand. Her fingers were warm and alive in mine.

"Dave." Her tone was pleading. "There are things you don't understand. I mean, maybe sometimes I do want to be closer, but not that way. I haven't had a real family ever and I'm just not sure, I mean I don't know what . . ."

She'd said she wanted to be closer and that was all I needed to hear. "See? I knew it! Come on," I wheedled.

She stood straighter, as if suddenly realizing my intentions, and jerked her hand from mine. "No," she said firmly.

"Why not? Nobody'll ever know."

I was desperate now and crazy enough not to care that my desperation showed. I was wild about this girl; her nearness to me was a torment.

"Oh, quit it." She was beginning to sound disgusted. "I said 'no' and I meant it."

"Every night in the lodge I can feel you over on the other side of the tarp," I began. Reining in my more reckless tendencies, I lowered my voice again. "Only a thin little tarp coming between us every night. I know you think about me too, I can see it in your face."

Actually, I was on thin ice here; I wasn't sure what I saw in her face, but I figured this was as good a guess as any. She'd tossed my hand away, so I raised it and cupped her chin.

"Every night," I insisted, in a low whisper. "It's like torture being that close to you, Lisa. Every night. You want to be near me, just like I want to be near you. Give in to it."

"No." She turned her head away, and to my fevered imagination she seemed to be waging some kind of internal battle. "Dave," she began finally, "I really like you. And I'd like us to be friends, maybe someday even closer than just friends. But you know this is wrong."

She'd said more than friends. I took this as encouragement. "Lisa, you know you want this," I said again. "Let's not lie there tonight wondering what might have been. Let's just do it."

There was a thread of steel in her voice when she replied. "This kind of stuff can't happen between us, Dave. You know it's wrong. We can be close in other ways, but you know this is wrong. And I know we're out in the bush and maybe you think things are different out here than in town, but they're really not. Besides, this is my life, Dave. Mine. I call the shots and I said no."

It was beginning to be obvious why the Aunts had been so unconcerned about a thought that had been bothering me lately, namely their questionable wisdom in bringing a young beautiful woman along on a camping trip with all us red-blooded males. Males whose virility and talents and whose nearness every day might lead a girl to thinking she'd kind of like having a man in her life. Me being the man, of course, since her choice was limited. I needn't have worried; Lisa obviously wasn't much given to falling for temptation.

All I wanted to do was hold her, kiss her; we didn't have to do anything more. Not today, anyway. "Come here," I whispered.

I reached out and slowly traced a finger down the line of her cheekbone until it came to rest on her lower lip. It was a sensual move, one I'd practised in my imagination, over and over, guaranteed to appeal to her softer side. Lisa's eyes closed slowly, her lashes like dark lace on her cheek. Her mouth was slightly open, revealing white teeth against red lips. Her eyes opened again, locked on mine, deep brown, liquid, soft. I moved my finger slowly over the curve of her lower lip, feeling its fullness, resting the tip on the inside of her mouth, reaching out for the point of her tongue.

The beautiful white teeth snapped shut with a sudden ferocity that left me panting for air.

"Ow!" I wrenched my crushed finger from her mouth and she smiled sweetly.

"I said 'no,'" she told me. "Didn't you hear me?"

"Well then, when? When can we?" I didn't care anymore how stupid or young I sounded. All that masculine-wiles stuff went straight out the window in my desperation. There was only one thing in the world I wanted, and I had to know when I was going to get it.

"Dave!" she sounded exasperated. "We're not going to 'do it,' and you know that! And you know why. Or, you should know why. You've got to think . . ." She left the rest unspoken. "That's not why I'm here, Dave," she said.

I glared at her. The tears in the back of my eyes were only partly caused by my throbbing finger.

"You left teeth marks!"

"You should know better!" Her voice was hot with anger. "I can't believe you'd even try this kind of stuff on me!"

"If it wasn't me, if it was some other guy, you wouldn't be so insulted. What's so terrible about me? I mean, I know I'm a bit younger than you, but . . ."

"There's nothing terrible about you," she interrupted. Stamping a foot in frustration, she whistled for Thor. "It's getting cold," she said in a voice that was chillier than the air. "I'm frozen. Don't try this on me again. I don't care how desperate you are."

Thor bounded up then and hurled himself against her in a fit of affection. She laughed and staggered back a step or two, and that seemed to restore her good humour.

"Come on, now." She finally transferred her attention from her dog back to me. "If we're going to be roommates we better learn to get along. Let's be friends, OK?"

"Friends? Right! And I can't come near you, right? And we aren't ever going to do anything more than shake hands at your wedding or something, right?" I realized too late that this wasn't coming out as sophisticated as I'd hoped.

"Well, I want more than that," I continued, "and so do you, so why are we letting all this other stuff get in our way?

"It could be so simple out here, Lisa." It'd work, I knew it would, if we wanted it bad enough and I definitely wanted it bad enough. "We could start our own lives, our own family. Little kids who'd love us and look up to us and we'd cook and hunt for them."

She could cook. I could make her happy. I admit, I was probably getting a little carried away, but at the time I really thought we could do all this. I could see Lisa and me married and happy together. A team. All I had to do was convince her; I could make her see.

"We could build a better shelter." It seemed imperative that she see the same vision I was seeing, and my voice got a little more strident. "Something more like a cabin, with a bed and a little kitchen. We could make it out of deadfall logs! There're tons of them around. Maybe we'd even figure out how to get running water and heat the water . . ."

I was dreaming out loud while she looked at me with something that I hoped was fondness in her eyes.

"Dave." She shook her head. "Stop it."

"What? We could, you know. We could do it all if we wanted to."

Lisa tossed her hair away from her eyes, put her hands on her hips and looked for all the world like one of those ticked-off mothers you see at the mall who have just too much lip from a toddler.

"This conversation is over!" Her voice was husky, but emphatic. "Now drop it. Don't even mention it to Jamie or the Aunts or anyone. It's too embarrassing."

And then she was gone, disappearing into the woods with Thor at her heels, heading back toward camp. The only sign my masculine wiles had made any impression on her was the string of snared animals she'd left behind.

Infallible Lisa, I sneered mentally as I picked up her string and added it to my load. Such a perfect person, and here she was not only neglecting her duties, but also adding to my own miserable load. There was still the wood to collect, I told myself, wallowing in my own pity – two carriers full in anticipation of the Aunts' mythical storm, and now I was stuck with her stupid rabbits to lug around, too.

Just see, I crabbed bitterly, if I save little old Lisa the best seat by the fire tonight. I kicked at a branch laden with snow. Just see, my girl, how much you're going to want me now that you can't have me anymore.

I had officially withdrawn my offer, and revenge, when it came, would be sweet. Nobody trampled on my feelings and got away with it. Someday she'd be begging – pleading for my forgiveness, realizing at long last what a great guy she'd given up, searching for the love she'd so carelessly tossed aside.

It was kind of sad, really, because in my mind's eye I could see myself just standing there, her abject apologies bouncing off my rugged frame. I'd never give in to her pleading, no matter how pathetic she became. Man of Steel, that would be me, and she'd have to bear the lonely burden of guilt for having made me that way.

The whole scenario nearly brought tears to my eyes. I swallowed hard, pushing any softer feelings back down where they couldn't get to me. The only thing I had left was pride, and I was hanging on to the shreds of it by my fingernails. She'd be sorry, I vowed, hacking my way through the brush. She could beg, she could cry, she could do a striptease right in front of me . . . my knees buckled at the mental image I'd conjured up and suddenly I was unmanned.

I purposely chose the most difficult, most overgrown path I could find and kicked and thrashed my way back to camp. My intention was to stiffen my resolve through exertion, and it worked because I was getting angrier with every step.

A willow branch whipped back at me as I forced my way through a growth of wild rose, thwacking me hard over the left eye and leaving a stinging welt behind. It hurt like crazy and it even bled a little, and it was all the reason I needed to swear and jump around and kick some of my anger away before entering camp.

CHAPTER FOURTEEN

THE SNOW BEGAN LATE that afternoon, drifting in silent little spirals through the light of the campfire. The wind followed a few hours later, wailing and twisting its tortured path out of the northeast accompanied by a frozen blast of air that blew with the demented howl of a ghostly coyote.

An unexpected little gust of chilly air had been our first indication the Aunts were right. Again. The wind slowly gained strength and brought with it a menacing chill, cutting through our clothes as we sat huddled before our little fire. It picked up force through dinner and the early evening until, as we straggled into the lodge for bed, it was beginning to rattle the high branches.

As the hours of darkness passed the wind grew in intensity, and with the approach of the main body of storm it howled through the woods with wild abandon, tossing trees and disturbing our sleep.

The tall-masted trees sighed mightily, heavy swinging branches rocking in a riotous way, lit by fitful glimpses of moonlight. Lower down, toward ground level, the force of the wind was blunted slightly by brush, but still working its way through the sheets of tarp covering the lodge, making them rattle and snap as if anxious to take flight.

Waking, I thought at first the noise was only part of my dream. I'd been lost somewhere bleak, riding a bike through a kind of sandstorm in a desert with the bike keeping up a steady whining complaint about my lack of riding skills and the fact its first owner had been far better looking. It left a sensation that was blurred but intense, as dreams tend to do, and when I finally did shake it off I discovered our makeshift lodge shuddering in its supports as the wind snaked its way through the clearing.

Lying there, I tried to retrieve parts of the dream, then gave up, and as the creak of tree limbs became louder I was suddenly filled with a strong sense of loneliness and fear.

"Anyone else awake?" I whispered.

"Go back to sleep, Dave." Dad's muffled voice came from the far wall. "Everything's OK. Just a change in the weather."

Some change. His voice was disembodied, floating, not exactly reassuring.

Jamie mumbled something in his sleep and laughed a loud incongruous laugh from somewhere far too close to my right ear for comfort. I wiggled a little farther away from him and spoke softly to Dad.

"What a goof," I whispered, referring to Jamie. "What a complete . . ."

"Go to sleep!"

The command came from behind the tarp barrier, over on the women's side of things. There was no point in arguing with either of the Aunts – I knew already who would come out the winner – so I fell silent, listening only half-awake to the gusts barreling through our forest.

It seemed to me a wind like that ought to have a name. It had at least as much personality as most people. Lisa's warm face crept into my thoughts and I forced her back. Although, I decided, maybe even the wind didn't have as much person-ality as Jamie. I glanced over to where he slept, oblivious to the racket around us.

Through the flimsy tarp a sleeping bag-covered hip thrust itself in my direction and I gingerly put out a hand and pushed back. I wasn't aware of the lay of the land over there, but there was a good chance the body I was touching was Lisa's. The thought made my throat thicken. I increased the pressure of my hand on the hip. Even through the layers of tarp and sleeping bag her body felt warm and giving.

Suddenly my shame knew no bounds. It could be Helen's hip I was caressing! Or Edith's! Withdrawing my hand, I rolled onto my other side. A rock seemed to settle somewhere in my head, and I lay there listening dully to the sounds of the storm.

The snow fell and the wind howled for two days and three nights. Halfway through the third night the edge of the screaming blast intensified briefly, then suddenly fell away to a sullen silence while the snow came down more thickly than ever.

During the course of the blizzard we'd been forced to venture outside once or twice a day, the guy ropes Dad had insisted upon tied around our waists, linking us to the lodge while we heated water for tea or checked on the horses.

It was a nerve-wracking time. We crouched for most of the day in our sleeping bags, whiling away the long hours of the tempest the best we could. Talk dropped off or was nonexistent while we waited for the storm to finally break and move on. For my own part, there seemed to be little to say. I was nursing a grudge against Dad for not including me in his thoughts and his life, against Lisa for being so immune to my charms, and against everyone else simply for being there. We were like a small herd of cranky bears forced to hibernate in the same small cave. Tempers, which were strained before, became worse. All we could do was huddle there in the semi-dark and mentally curse, at least in my own case, our stupidity in ever leaving home.

When the storm finally blew itself out we found our world covered in crusty, weirdly shaped snow carvings formed by the relentless wind. The temperature had taken a severe nosedive and only the driving force of Dad and the Aunts had ensured our keeping the coals of a small fire alive.

Dad was huddled over it now, tenderly feeding the dying embers, huffing gentle puffs of air over any warm spots in order to get the heat moving through his carefully constructed pile of dried pine needles and tiny twigs before adding larger fuel.

"Get some of that snow off the top of the lodge," Edith commanded as I edged my way past Lisa and her dog.

Thor's ribs were beginning to show. The steady diet of squirrel and rabbit was beginning to wear on him as well as the rest of us. Lisa's face had lost its original plumpness and was reduced to planes and angles.

"Come on, move!" Edith urged. She waved a long supple pine branch in my face. "Lodge might collapse," she said. "The snow is heavy. Use this to sweep."

A storm of this magnitude meant only one thing, I figured, and that was that life was going to get a lot tougher before it got any easier. The mundane, time-consuming chores, which are part of camping and even kind of fun in warm weather, would now become a finger and bone-numbing form of torture.

Keeping the fire lit and burning solid was number one priority and getting the horses fed and as comfortable as possible was number two. Then came dish-washing, cooking, fetching water, dumping water, melting snow and just taking care of one's own bodily functions.

Because of the extreme cold and the piled-up drafts all around, a guy could easily envision himself pinned helplessly to some snowbank by a frozen arc of piss, like an unfortunate bug pinned to a sheet of white paper. I stood and relieved myself behind the dense line of brush designated as the men's station. How the women managed to cope under conditions like these boggled the mind. The women's outdoor facilities had been chosen for proximity to camp and for privacy. There was a strictly enforced no-trespassing rule governing each area, and the space in between was a virtual no man's land.

The sight of a bobbing red pom-pom moving along past my line of brush jerked me out of my thoughts.

"Hey, Jamie!" I called, zipping up again. "Hey, wait a minute, man!"

When the Aunts divvied up chores that morning, Jamie had drawn water duty while Dad and I had been sent off to re-tether the horses in an area where they could more easily break through the snow to whatever grass and herbage lay beneath. We were finished, but Jamie appeared to be still hard at it. He had a bucket in each hand for balance as he wove his way through drifts along the rough little path he'd broken.

"What's going on?" I asked conversationally, falling into step behind him. It suddenly struck me as odd that I couldn't remember Jamie having spoken much lately. We hadn't had a conversation in days, not since well before the storm. In fact, I'd hardly noticed his presence, which should have prompted a warning flag, but hadn't. "How much more water do you have to bring in?"

He stopped short and handed a bucket back to me, not that I'd asked for one. "Gotta wash," he explained. "This is dirty work, this camping. A man's gotta get clean."

"OK," I said slowly. Here was a new facet to Jamie's character. It seemed safest to simply agree with him.

"How much water do the Aunts want you to bring in? I could give you a hand since old Silent Sam and I are finished with the horses."

I dodged a low branch laden with snow and walked right into Jamie, who had spun around to face me.

"I gotta get clean!" he said loudly. He seemed to be under the impression I'd gone deaf. Motioning wildly with his free hand, he imitated a guy taking a shower, scrubbing under his arms.

"Clean!" he hollered again. "They aren't going to let me sell Coke to the cuties if I'm not clean, are they?"

"No, probably not."

"Well then, I gotta go wash up."

Not, that he couldn't use a bath – we all could – but this obsession with personal hygiene was a new one for Jamie. All that quiet dark time spent in the lodge seemed, in his case, to have been squandered on dangerous dreams of bubble baths and Jacuzzis.

"How is washing up now going to help you get a job next summer?" I reasoned. "You're only going to get dirty again. What if we're not even home by next summer?"

Jamie dropped his bucket into the spring and hauled it out again. Warm sulphurous water lipped over the sides as he propped it upright in the snow. The ice had closed in a little more on the lake, but the pool itself was unaffected by the change in weather, although some of the small clumps of wildflowers struggling to survive at the edge of the warm water now had a light dusting of snow over them.

"Campfire ash everywhere," Jamie commented, not answering my question. "See my fingernails?"

He pulled off a mitt and held his hand out to me, palm down. "Look at that! I might never get them clean again."

Jamie took a step closer, glanced over his shoulder, and in a hoarse whisper added, "Look in my hair, under my hat. Go ahead, take a look."

I pretended to glance at his head. He was getting creepier by the minute.

"See any?"

"See any what?" I wasn't sure what I was looking for.

"Bugs! There's bugs in my hair! See any?"

"No." I wondered how long he'd been this way. He'd been quieter than usual for a while now, but it had seemed such a blessing at the time that I don't think any of us had chosen to question it.

"I can't see any bugs in your hair," I offered. "Maybe you should take your hat off once in a while and let the fresh air get in there. Maybe your head would feel better."

"And freeze? Are you kidding? It's way too cold to take my hat off." Jamie swung the other bucket into the water and watched it fill.

"I'll drown 'em," he muttered. "I'll drown the bloodsucking little buggers."

Pulling at his jacket, he toppled over into the bank of snow, while I made a grab for the sinking bucket. By the time I got it propped safely alongside the first one Jamie was tugging at his boots and socks. Before I could do more than holler his name he was lying there nude in the snow. It was a sight I wished I'd never seen. My eyes would never be the same. I mean, I'd heard of male bonding, but this was ridiculous.

"Aw, Jamie! For crying out loud, man, you're gonna freeze! Get your clothes back on. That's disgusting!"

He stood and plunged suddenly into the hot spring.

"Die, you little bugs!" he screamed. "Die!"

He scrunched down, submersing himself, hair and all into the warm water.

"Jamie, look." I tried reasoning with him, trying not to actually look at him, when he emerged again, dripping wet. "You don't even have a towel. Here, dry off with your scarf. You're scaring me, man. You're really weird, you know that?"

"Me? Weird?" Jamie stood there, the cold air like a knife around his wet body. "You think I'm weird? Well, man, at least I'm not in love with my sister."

One thing about Jamie, when he starts raving he raves and at the same time, his natural state is one of constant gassing about one random thing or another, so not making sense in Jamie's case is his home-field advantage. It's one way to keep people off-guard. He doesn't have a sister, so not being in love with her was relatively simple, but there was zero point in arguing with him. I was more concerned with covering him up again. Starting with his pants and shirt. The length of his body was quaking now in uncontrollable waves as he began trying to dry himself with his long scraggly hunk of woolen scarf.

"At least I have more sense than that," he cried. His eyes were fixed on mine in a wild stare.

"What sister?" I said, trying to humour him while I grabbed at the end of his trailing scarf. "You don't have a sister, Jamie."

I wanted to get him dressed again, mostly so he wouldn't freeze to death, but if I'm being honest, then even more for my own mental health, but he kept whipping the tail end of that striped scarf around, slapping me around the face with it. I was beginning to wonder if I could run back to camp and get help before he became a human Popsicle, but he was trembling from the cold and he still hadn't begun to get himself dressed. If I left him standing here naked he might be dead before I got back.

"No, but you've got a sister," he was saying coyly as I pulled his shirt around his shoulders and began buttoning it. "It's illegal to go after your sister, man."

He was hallucinating, getting me confused with Les or somebody. I'd never seen anyone actually lose their mind before, and it was beginning to dawn on me that

Jamie was more than a little scary. He seemed to have lost touch with reality, and since the only crazy people I'd ever seen were in the movies, I knew I was completely out of my comfort zone here. I needed help and Jamie needed it even more.

"Jamie, quit talking and get dressed." My breath came out in puffs of white frost as I struggled to lift his leg and pull his pants over it. "Shut up for a while, and get some clothes on before you catch something."

Like pneumonia, I thought, or Mad Jamie disease.

"Those Aunts," he said, chuckling. "Man, what kidders! Who would have guessed they could keep a secret that long." He placed a finger alongside his nose and wobbled in closer to me. "Remember I told you not to trust them? Remember I said they were weird? Heard 'em talking, man. Heard 'em telling her to be patient. Your Dad'll tell it all when he's ready. Ha!"

He struck a goofy pose and collapsed giggling in the snow.

"Tell me what? Dad'll tell me what?" Something hard rose up inside me, hurting my chest. A nameless thing I didn't want to look at too closely was starting to appear in my head. My mouth was dry with apprehension. "I don't have a sister."

"Sure you do!" he said in triumph, pounding a friendly fist on my shoulder. "A half-sister, at least. And Lisa's a bit of a pain sometimes, but she's OK. You'll learn to like her."

My heart seemed to suddenly stop.

"Tell me what the Aunts said," I ordered, a trifle breathlessly.

"Which one? Aunt Helen?"

I resisted an urge to strike him. "Yeah," I agreed, "tell me what Aunt Helen said."

Jamie seated himself comfortably on a nearby rock and crossed one leg over the other, as if presiding over some kind of warped tea party. "Well, your mom had Lisa before she met your dad. Way, way back," he said, gesturing behind him and nearly falling off his rock in the process.

"It was my uncle," he confided, "a real nogoodnik if there ever was one. Even the Aunts didn't trust him. Your Mom went back to the city and she got Lisa out of some foster place, but your Mom was a little screwed up herself, no offence man, and she got back with my rotten uncle or some other guy or something . . ."

Jamie was wandering now, obviously less than clear about what had really happened. He trembled with a huge shudder.

"Everyone dies from the cold," he whispered through blue lips. "It hurts. It's so cold."

I grabbed at his hat and pulled it down over his ears. He was pulling at his clothes again, but I yanked his arms out and shoved his mitts more firmly onto his hands.

"It's so cold," he moaned again. "A person could just curl up and die of the cold."

"Come on." I shoved my arm around his body and tried to pull him upright. "Time to go home, Jamie."

"Home?" A light film of sweat covered his face, but he was shaking from chills at the same time.

"Yeah. We'll get you warm again, OK?"

"OK."

It was nice to have him become so docile, but it would have been nicer if he'd been able to walk on his own. His legs buckled spasmodically as I half-carried, half-pushed him up the path toward camp.

Once I got him back we propped him on a log by the fire with his sleeping bag wrapped around his shoulders. The Aunts and Lisa spent the rest of that day pouring hot tea laced with our precious sugar down his throat, while whatever bug he'd picked up worked its way through his system.

As for me, I spent the rest of that day being a good little camper boy, chopping extra wood and washing dishes, feeding the horses and generally keeping out of everyone's way in a futile attempt to believe Jamie had got the facts wrong as usual and Dad hadn't purposely kept the knowledge of my sister and Mom from me. Because there was no way even Dad would do that.

He'd have found some way to tell me, no matter how hard it was for him to talk about it because nobody would do that to another person – sit back silently and watch them fall madly in love with someone who happened to be their half-sister.

CHAPTER FIFTEEN

THE CAMPFIRE WAS DYING. Only embers remained from the fire we'd built up to cook the evening stew – a concoction made by Helen from leftover rabbit snared before the storm, served with a chunk of bannock. I shoved the end of a long log into the centre of the fire pit and watched as it blazed up, lighting the circle of tired faces surrounding it.

Jamie was now scarily sick. He sat there huddled by the fire, moaning every once in a while as another wave of pain swept through his joints. Clutching at his head, he complained through chattering teeth about the headache raging through his skull until I could almost feel the pain myself.

The grooves on each side of Dad's face had deepened during these last weeks, from a combination of stress and lack of proper food, until they seemed carved into his skin. I watched him as he sat, the light from the flickering fire giving fitful glimpses of his expression, an expression that told me nothing.

And the women, who had seemingly signed some sort of zero-compliance pact amongst themselves, were quiet as usual, even though life was almost impossibly tough and getting worse by the day.

Lisa sat next to Dad, her chin propped in both palms, watching intently as he stripped the bark from a thin stick in preparation for drawing. In the time we'd been gone Dad had never once admitted to missing his art. He'd seemed intent, for the most part, on simply surviving from one day to the next. Now, for some reason that none of us questioned, the urge to put things down on paper had returned. He took one of Pete's letters from its envelope, tossed the letter aside unread and slit the envelope along three sides to form a blank sheet of paper.

He collected small piles of ash from different areas in the fire pit. I watched Lisa as she watched Dad carefully place each in a separate heap on a flat rock, then fill his tin mug with water and plunk it down in the center of the ash piles. Using the blade of his pocket knife, he sharpened the peeled stick to make a point at one end, then blunted the thicker end for use as a smoothing, shading tool.

Dad dipped the tip of his ring finger into the water and smeared it through one of the piles of ash, making a sort of paste, then used the pointed end of his stick to draw a series of lines of varying thickness diagonally across one corner of the paper.

He drew slowly, Lisa's eyes following the patterns as he made them. Appearing slowly out of the maze of lines was the old truck seat from the porch back home. It was a sagging green and blue plaid bench seat from the wreck of an old '57 Chevy that Dad and I used as a seat in the summertime where we could sit and watch the world.

"I knew you wouldn't be able to hold out." I broke the silence, customary now after the day's chores had been done and dinner finished. Leaning farther toward the fire, I tossed a couple of pine cones into the middle of the flames and watched as they sizzled and cracked. Even I could pick up the note of sarcastic triumph in my voice as I added, "I knew you'd have to start drawing again."

The pause that followed seemed endless. Lisa brushed her bangs aside, sat a little straighter and glanced again at Dad's sketch.

"I asked him to teach me to draw," she said quietly.

A muscle in Dad's jaw twitched at the sound of her voice, but he stayed silent.

"How do you draw clouds like we had today?" Lisa asked Dad. "The dark kind that are even darker when the sun breaks through?"

Dad took a moment, then answered slowly. "It's more a matter of leaving things out than drawing things in," he said.

Wetting a fingertip, he blotted up some darker ash and smeared it quickly onto the page. He shaded with a variety of ash grays, leaving one untouched place in the center of the page a stark white to suggest the sun's rays.

"See how it works?" he asked. "Try it yourself."

Lisa took the proffered sheet of paper and began a tentative sketch of her own. Her dark hair drifted across one cheek while she concentrated on her drawing, and I felt a familiar tugging at my heart. A tugging I shoved brutally to one side.

"You ought to comb your hair once in a while, you look like a mess," I said in a voice that sounded harsh even to my own ears.

For a moment the words hung there in the silence, seemingly unheard.

"Were you talking to me?" Lisa sounded confused more than hurt.

"Yeah. I mean, a girl ought to at least comb her hair once in a while."

The Aunts, sitting on the far side of the fire mending a pair of mittens, glanced at each other, but remained silent.

"I don't think my hair is any of your business," Lisa answered. She held her drawing up and squinted at it in the dim light of the fire.

"Maybe we should continue your lesson tomorrow," Dad said, "when the light's a little better."

"No, let's keep going. What did I do wrong?"

"Well," he was whittling at another stick as he spoke, "sometimes it helps to have a lighter touch. You can always add to it later on, but you can't take things off the paper once they're on."

"Not only that, but you look like a slob half the time."

Ignoring me wasn't an option anymore. I was determined to be heard, the words coming out of my mouth coated with a bitterness I couldn't disguise any longer. They'd been treating me like I didn't exist long enough. Nobody seemed to ever take my feelings into consideration. It was like they thought I was made out of clay or some unfeeling hunk of wood or something. They were wrong. It hurt to think of Lisa as even a half-sister, and hurt even more to think that absolutely everybody else knew about our relationship before I did. It meant they'd been discussing it behind my back. I hated the thought of being the topic of other people's conversations.

"It's OK for a guy to look like a slob," I said conversationally. I couldn't seem to stop myself now that I'd started. "But it's really awful for a girl. I'm surprised your mother never told you that. Thank god you haven't put on weight, because if you were fat, too . . ."

"Dave!" Dad got to his feet slowly. His hands were trembling, but his eyes were level. "Knock it off, right now."

"Knock it off!" I jeered in return. "Sure, why not? Why not just knock everything off? That's how we handle our problems, isn't it? We just knock it off! Well, let's just knock off these stupid camping tricks, and the lodge and the horses while we're at it. Just knock off the whole dumb experiment!"

"What's the matter with you?" Dad seemed almost too exhausted to talk at all. "Dave," he said, "just calm down, son. Cool it."

"Cool nothin'!" My voice was beyond my own control now. Any restraint I might have once been able to exert was totally gone now. "I'm finished being 'cool' about things, Dad! Thanks for telling me about Lisa," I added sarcastically. "Thanks one whole helluva lot, Dad!"

I stood now and faced him, my hands clenched into fists. It surprised me for an instant to realize I was as tall as he was now. Nearly as heavy, too. For two cents I'd have clocked him one right then and there.

"Thanks," I continued, and to my own horror, my voice cracked. "Mom's dead and Lisa's here instead and nobody told me a God damn thing. Thanks once again."

I kicked out violently at one of the poles supporting the lodge, a substitute for kicking out at Dad. "I'm sick of this. I'm starving! I'd give my life right now for a french fry. For one single greasy little french fry! I'd crawl over broken glass for a pizza. Cheese. Salami. Anything! Even a glass of milk!"

"We can't have those things out here, Dave," Dad said, pointing out the obvious in such a frustratingly flat tone I nearly came undone.

"Well, then, maybe we shouldn't be out here!" I shot back. I turned and hurled a kick at the campfire, scattering ash and coals, making sparks fly across the dark sky. "Maybe we should be back in civilization where people can choose their lives without having stuff forced down their throats by dictators like you!"

I'd gone so far now there was no point anymore in backing down. Dad was hurt by what I'd said, and that knowledge made me even angrier. How dare he be hurt after what he'd put me through? Right now I hated him so much, hated the camp, hated Lisa and the Aunts and hated the lies they had between them. It was the lies most of all. I hated the lies.

"This is ridiculous, man," I heard myself ranting. "Jamie's gone bush-crazy on us. I'm starving to death, I'm skin and bones and you know it and so is everyone else. Having Lisa around all the time is nothing but a pain."

Dad held up one hand for quiet and I yelled back. "You knew what I felt about her! You knew and you still didn't tell me the truth! What's the matter with you?"

Lisa had her eyes on the paper in her lap, but she wasn't actually drawing anymore, just looking down. The Aunts regarded me with great interest, like some odd insect under a microscope, and Jamie, since he was nowhere to be seen, was probably off at the pool washing invisible germs from his hands.

"Even the horses are getting thin and don't have any energy. Even Stanley." I knew how much Dad thought of his horse. "They need better food. Maybe the Indians in the old days lived like this and maybe they didn't, but these aren't the old days anymore, Dad!"

It was all I could do to keep my lips from trembling and breaking into sobs like some little kid. Dad doesn't like big displays of emotion of any kind, happy or sad. I knew I'd lose him for sure if I broke down.

"These are just these days, Dad," I finished as quietly as I could. "We just have to live our lives. We have to be able to talk to each other. You have to be able to talk to me. We just have to do the best we can."

He was sitting there, silent as usual, his eyes not giving anything away. Poker-playing Dad. The Great Stone Face. He was probably wondering if it was possible to slip a pair of hobbles on me, maybe a gag or two to shut me up for a while and get me out of his hair.

"The horses need grass," Dad said finally in a voice whose calmness was like pouring gasoline on a fire to me. "In a few weeks they'll get a good feed. Spring is on the way."

I didn't wait for him to finish his thought. "In a few weeks some of them will be dead and you know it! The alfalfa cubes are nearly gone and the grass they find is old and mouldy and they use more energy digging it than they get from eating it."

I waited for him to respond, to say something that would fix everything and give me some kind of reason to keep going. He was doodling on his paper. I wasn't even sure he was listening anymore, and that's when I completely lost it.

"Jamie needs some kind of help, Dad. Are you gonna wait until we're all sick and half-insane? Maybe you plan to wait until a horse or two dies and then we can skin them and eat them and for entertainment we can sit around the campfire at night and watch Jamie go crazy! What if one of the Aunts gets sick? They're pretty old, you know. What'll you do then? Pray to some old dead Indian spirits or something?"

"David, be quiet for a minute," Dad commanded. "Just let me speak, OK?"

"You had your chance to speak," I sputtered. "You had a million chances. You could have told me about Mom, you could have told me about Lisa, but no, not you, you had to go into one of your famous silent routines. You could have trusted me!"

The shock on his face made me turn away. I'd gone too far. Bringing up Mom's name was always too far.

From far off there was a buzzing noise, but I was so wired it barely registered.

"So we proved we can live out here. So what?" Sometimes I just don't know when to shut up. "All we're doing is barely surviving. Where's the point in that?"

The hard lump in my throat finally stopped me. Dad's face seemed to age right in front of my eyes. He'd been losing weight, and the beard he'd been growing looked patchy, as if he didn't have any excess energy left to put into growing it. It wasn't as easy to see the weight loss on him since he's skinny to begin with, but by the light of the fire it looked as if his bones would saw through the skin on his face.

I turned and stumbled back a step toward the lodge.

"Dave!" he called in a half-hearted way. "Come on back here, son."

The buzzing had become louder, more insistent, and as he spoke Dad turned in the direction of the noise. Pete. It hit me like a ton of bricks. Pete was on his way to check up on us to make sure we were still alive after the storm.

And of course, he and Dad would argue. He'd push and prod and tell Dad to go back home to his painting and his life and Dad would become more stubborn than ever. We'd never leave. Never. Dad would probably move us all to some godforsaken spot even Pete had never heard of.

I couldn't take any more of it. Taking advantage of their inattention, I crept through the lodge opening and grabbed at my sleeping bag where it lay in its little sack, then backed quietly through the opening and snuck off down the darkened deer trail.

CHAPTER SIXTEEN

When the rain began falling later that night I was already several miles from camp and, in more ways than one, I found myself heading in a direction I'd never gone before. Not only was I physically lost, but also any hard-earned pointers about survival in the great outdoors that I'd inadvertently picked up from hanging around the Aunts seemed to have vacated the premises. My brain felt fried, numb, like a frozen chunk of baloney. The territory I found myself covering was unfamiliar, and when it got too dark to travel farther I bedded down in a thicket of willow and wild rose, whose bare and tangled branches only partly protected me from the damp.

The tracks around the brush I was huddled down in had been cloven-hoofed or at least small enough to represent no threat to my personal safety; that much knowledge at least remained from the Aunts. There was still a lingering dread of finding myself cuddled up next to a bear or cougar or even a coyote, which I was finding it hard to ignore, but the fight with Dad had exhausted me to the extent that even my fears, along with the occasional drop of rain in my face, were unable to keep me awake for long.

As my eyes finally drifted shut, a nameless terror bubbled up, oozing around the edges of consciousness. I pushed it back. The anger was still too fresh and strong to be intimidated and I was too exhausted both physically and mentally to do any thinking at all. Repercussions and recriminations and the paying of dues could wait.

The rain gradually increased in intensity, the drops large and sullen, plopping down through my makeshift shelter, soaking the outer skin of my sleeping bag. I yanked my hat down hard around my ears, pulled the bag up over my head and cocooned myself for the night.

First morning light would find me gone, I vowed sleepily, long before anyone had the chance to track me down. For the time being I knew only that I had to be away from them all, no matter what the consequences. It was physically impossible for me to sit at the fire, surrounded by the Aunts, Dad and Lisa, and act like nothing unusual had happened. That ability to fake well-being and pretend nothing had changed was beyond me. My feelings were too raw. It felt as though nerve endings were sticking out through my skin, tingling and itching with every passing breeze. Every inch of me felt bruised.

———————

Next morning I was up and on my way before the sun had fully risen. My legs were cramped from sleeping in a tightly wound knot all night and I was cold, hungry and stiff, but none of it mattered. I was free, and the accumulated anger and frustration of the last months were all the fuel I needed to keep me moving.

After the forced companionship of being surrounded by others for the past weeks, the woods now seemed silent and eerie. The only sign of life other than mine was the constant chirping of sparrows. It almost seemed as if all other animals and birds had disappeared, leaving behind only huge flocks of the little scrappy brown birds. Their chatty high-pitched voices kept me company as I pulled my damp bag out of the slushy snow and packed it under one arm before beginning to beat my way again through the bush.

The wind gusting down from the western slopes of the mountains was warm and moist, smelling of spring and new beginnings, and it filled me with energy. A handful of dried-up saskatoon berries from the summer before, washed down with a few mouthfuls of melted snow, made for a meagre breakfast, but even that small amount of food seemed to ease the worst of the hunger pangs, and my legs suddenly felt stronger and more able to carry me where I needed to go.

The clouds scudding across the sky were obviously still full of humidity but moving too quickly this morning to drop their load. Their grey-white colour and their shape, that of fat, dirty sponges, gave them away as moisture-laden, but the warm breeze meant any snow falling from them would turn to rain before hitting the ground. At least it would so long as the air stayed warm from the west, which was not a thing I would bet any money on, judging from my previous experience along these foothills. It was OK, though, because as long as the weather was milder I'd be able to keep warm myself and travel more easily. Or at least, that's what I thought at the time, rookie that I still was.

The one factor I knew I couldn't ignore was Pete and his snowmobile. And the horses. Anyone from camp was able to move a lot faster than I could, and that realization made me hustle. There was no doubt in my mind they'd be starting to look for me. Even if he was still raging from last night, I knew Dad would be worried. It would be humiliating to be dragged back by Dad and Pete like some little wayward kid. I'd go back or not go back in my own good time.

Thinking of camp brought Lisa to mind, and once again I cursed my own stupidity. When I got tired of cursing myself, I cursed all of them. All the people who knew everything I didn't know and had kept the knowledge from me on purpose, it seemed, to embarrass me and make me look like a fool. Thoughts of the scene with Lisa ran through my mind in a relentless loop that only served to make me blush with regret and renewed rage before I shoved them into the back of my head where they belonged.

I'd been making good time, not following any particular trail, just heading where the spirit led me and following the lower edge of what seemed to be a massive chunk of granite, but it seemed maybe I should get an idea of where I was going and start making a bit of a plan. Stopping for a moment to catch my breath and take a look around, I sagged back against the rock where the warmth of sun remained, and realized suddenly the big drawback for those who depended on either horses or snowmobiles to get around. Neither of them is effective in dense bush and neither of them is any good on a straight climb upwards, either. I grinned, cocked my head back to look upwards and slapped a hand on the trunk of a weedy little poplar.

"Up we go," I said aloud.

CHAPTER SEVENTEEN

FTER WHAT SEEMED like a week later, but was really only a couple of hours, I stopped, out of breath, to assess my escape efforts. The climb I'd chosen was a lot harder than it looked from the base of that skinny little poplar.

It had started as a fairly steep ascent through dense brush that ended again at the base of another nearly vertical cliff. I'd been able to scramble up this far without too much trouble, but some of the handholds ahead of me now were nothing more than bare rock, and getting a finger or toe lodged in them wasn't going to be easy, especially when my personal comfort zone mainly involved sitting in a chair in front of a computer with the heat on and a fridge full of food only a few steps away. I shook my head hard and banished the mental picture I'd inadvertently conjured. Fridges, stoves, even four walls and a roof were a long way off and no good to me now.

Heights. I'd never been a big fan of heights. Even the top side of the teeter-totter when I was little was a major stretch. I'd been known to descend into ever-increasing paroxysms of nervous hysteria as a four-year-old out on that playground. It had taken me years to live it down. In a town as small as ours is all those little traits from childhood are nearly impossible to escape. Some jerk with an axe to grind is always bringing them up, hoping and usually succeeding to embarrass you in front of some girl he's trying to impress.

"Don't look down, don't look down." I muttered a mantra in a sing-song voice and forced my eyes upward, pausing for a few minutes on a narrow ledge and wedging myself back against the cliff face to consider the possibilities. The sheer rock face that I was forced to tackle next was one that didn't get much sun this time of year. Clumps of snow clung to every little crevice and bulge. The snow would be slick underneath where the rock had warmed a little; of that I was certain. Falling was a distinct possibility. So was breaking my neck.

Then, from far off, came the unmistakable buzz of a motor. Pete. And Dad. Not to mention, Lisa, the Aunts and Jamie, all of them brimming with various levels of accusations and pity. It was hard to say which I dreaded facing most – the accusing wrath of Dad, Pete's well-meaning advice or the pitying look in Lisa's dark eyes. With no time left to make an intelligent choice I fought off a surge of panic and chose to go up.

Raw fear nearly made me gag every time I gave myself the luxury of actually thinking about what I was doing. But thinking would be my downfall. I knew this. I also knew there was no way in this life I was going back with them like some kid acting like a little jerk. Concentrating on anger, on how I'd been deceived, would be my hope.

Swallowing hard to take the edge of my panic, I took a couple of seconds to figure out my next move. The climb upward would be tough, especially since I already possessed an inborn horror of heights. Don't think, I repeated in a kind of monotonous lullaby, don't think, don't think . . . And then I spotted it. It was difficult to make out, even harder to memorize, but there was a distinct wavering fault line made up of little ledges and small scrubby twigs to grab onto winding its way up the cliff face. For the first time, I realized I really could do this. With that realization came a new surge of energy and confidence.

Dad and Pete would have to ditch their transportation to follow me up the rock face, or break trail through heavy wet snow until they found another way to the top. It would take time, a lot of time, and energy for them to follow me.

My sleeping bag, in its little sack, had been looped through the belt of my jeans, banging against my leg with every move I made. It was bound to throw me off balance during the climb when I'd need to concentrate all my movements to keep from falling. At the same time, I was intensely grateful to the Aunts for their insistence on good housekeeping habits. If my bag hadn't been stowed away in its sack when I grabbed it on my way out of camp, I'd have had six feet of flopping goose down to lug around instead of a neat little package complete with carrying string.

Quaking a little at the thought of what lay ahead, I untied my boots and looped their laces through the string of the sleeping bag, then slung the cord over my head experimentally. Not bad. With the collar of my jacket as padding, the string was only a slight weight against my throat.

The snarl of Pete's snowmobile was closer now, eating up the miles I'd put between myself and the others. I wondered, as I yanked off my heavy socks and stuffed them in a pocket, if Dad was on Stanley covering different territory or behind Pete on the machine. The realization that they could easily have found last night's resting spot made me jumpy. I flexed my feet, pale white and already chilly, against the frozen chunks of moss under them, trying to keep my toes from curling automatically away from the icy ground.

Standing again, I reached tentatively with my left hand for the first little ledge, then dropped down again and took off my sheepskin mitts, shoving them into another pocket. I felt like one of the packhorses, laden down with boots and clothes, but the various ledges and cracks which I'd mapped out in advance as my route were going to be tough enough to hold onto without mitts and socks in the way.

Starting out again, my fingernails dug into the rough granite and I found my first toehold at the same time, pulling the weight of my body away from the safety of the ledge, against the cliff and letting out a pent-up sigh at the same time. I was on my way.

The sound of Pete's vehicle receded to a background buzz while I pushed my way up the cliff, concentrating only on my next hand and toe hold, and unaware of conditions outside my own little bubble of activity. It was a long hour later when I found myself clinging like a fly to a wall, 30 feet or more from ground level, gasping for breath and sweating like a maniac, with nowhere to go.

My head felt twice its normal size, the blood pounding hot in my ears. The sleeping bag and boots were now a dead weight across my neck where the cord from the bag had slipped off my jacket collar, biting into the skin, their combined weight making a stranglehold against my throat. What had once seemed like such a great idea was now cutting off circulation and leaving me light-headed. My arms and legs trembled with the effort of keeping my body vertical on the barren rock face.

The scream of the engine loomed suddenly closer. They were narrowing my lead. I was trapped. Desperately I yanked at the cord around my neck, frantic to get some relief from the pressure, to be able to think clearly for a second. Holding myself stiff against the icy rock, one hand wedged into a narrow gap, my toes stiff from cold, but on relatively solid little outcroppings, I pulled against the weight of the string and then gasped in a long wheeze of cold air. Which was precisely the moment the knot on the cord gave way, and all I could do was watch as my bag and boots, parting company halfway down, bounced and tumbled their way to the heavy brush at the cliff base.

Pete's engine cut off and the sudden silence was almost as shocking as an unexpected blast of thunder on a hot day. All I could hear now was the sound of my own raspy breath, blood pounding harshly through my skull, and the thud of my heart.

I stayed where I was, plastered against the rock, searching the brush below for the red cover of my sleeping bag, and then, as the sound of Pete's voice hollering my name ricocheted off the mountains, I forced myself to look up again.

The route I'd mentally mapped out when resting on the ledge seemed to have vanished; nothing looked the same up here as it did from below. When I was clutched against the stone I couldn't even see the next finger-hold, let alone touch it. Either it had been a mirage or it had got up and walked away, but it definitely wasn't there anymore. I scrabbled my right hand around as far as I could reach, but I felt nothing but flat granular rock. Using my left and swinging it in a wide, slowly exploring arc, I finally found what I was so desperately searching for: a tiny crack in the granite.

By bringing my left foot up to knee level I wedged my toes onto a small outcrop, brushing the cap of snow off as I did. Using the toehold and bracing my weight with the other hand, I worked my fingers into the crumbly centre of the crack and, when it held, I breathed again. It was nice to know I wasn't going to follow my boots. Not yet, anyway.

Pete was excited, and though the actual words were blurred by distance I could tell he'd spotted my trail. All they had to do was follow my footprints in the snow, a task that took practically no brains at all. Even Jamie would be able to do it, and as Dad and Pete were no dopes when it came to the bush they'd be right underneath me in no time. I craned my neck to look up. The top of the cliff was tantalizingly close now; all I had to do was find some impossible way to make it up there. They'd hit a dead end where my tracks stopped at the base of the cliff, and I'd be free.

Cursing and sweating with effort I wedged my body closer, willing myself to hang on, pushing forward when every muscle screamed at me to relax and let go. My fingers and toes felt like raw meat; the rock had sandpapered the exposed skin, and the sweat flowing down made every scrape itch and sting.

And then, when the urge to just let go, just give in, was at its strongest, my hand reached out for one more hold and grabbed instead a long twiny root. I was there. It was the top. One more serious effort and I'd managed to tussle my way up and over. By the time Dad and Pete reached the base of the cliff I was sprawled on my belly looking down at them.

CHAPTER EIGHTEEN

ONE THING HARD WORK DOES for you is clear the brain waves. That night I huddled, without a sleeping bag or boots, at the base of an ancient spruce tree. The branches sagged low to the ground, meeting the snow banked by the wind near its base and providing a sort of tent at the trunk. With a few boughs pulled down to make a bed I was almost reasonably comfortable. Except for my feet, which were wet and cold from hiking around in only my socks, and my stomach, which was achingly empty.

Infuriated thoughts about Lisa and her deception had mellowed under the awful strain of the day. She still seemed like a beautiful prize I'd somehow lost. The resentment still burned, but my rage at her had eased a little, and was instead focused even more acutely on Dad. Pete and the Aunts were a part of it, too, since they had known the whole story, but Pete and the Aunts were not my family. Dad was my family, and even though my fury at losing Lisa was starting to cool, the anger aimed at him was as hot as ever.

When I closed my eyes I could still see Lisa's eyes shining with reproach and something else, while her mouth turned down at the edges in disappointment. She had a great mouth. Especially when she wasn't pissed at me. When she smiled she was beautiful. Envisioning her face made me feel slightly less alone, up to the point where fatigue made me a little sloppy and her face morphed into Aunt Edith's lined and worn visage. I started awake again.

It was beginning to dawn on me through my haze of fury and disappointment that Lisa had no doubt had a rough life all along. Rougher than Jamie's or mine. More like some of those town kids I knew who hang out anywhere they can and never seem to want to go home. It was hard to picture what she must have had to endure in the foster care system or what her relationship with our mother might have been, but the fact she hadn't screamed or smacked me that day in the bush was starting to cast her in a new light. A better light, but still a bittersweet one. It wasn't going to be easy thinking about her being with some other guy someday, but at the same time it occurred to me she might have a whack of boyfriends in her life, but she'd only have one brother. We could maybe start to build on that. Maybe it would be nice having someone else to deal with Dad once in a while. It wasn't much, but it was something to hang onto, and at this point I was ready to take what I could get.

I dozed off that night thinking of her, my mind slowly opening to the possibilities of having an actual sibling. It wasn't anything I'd even imagined before. Dad and I had made a compact unit between the two of us for so many years now that the thought of a third person in our little family had never entered into it. Having a sister wasn't absolutely impossible to imagine, though, and maybe even a little comforting.

It was two nights later that I saw Mom.

Sleep was my way of escaping the circumstances I found myself in, and even though it was too cold and scary to ever sleep really well, it seemed that every chance I got over the next couple of days I dropped down and dozed. I'd stagger on a ways every time I heard that distant whine of Pete's snow machine, and then I'd scrape a little pit in some snowbank under a random tree, drop down, think of Lisa's eyes and try to rest a little. It was exhausting. All of it.

For what seemed like all my life but was really only a couple of days, my only thoughts had been to find a place to hide and spend the night after scrabbling a few dried berries off a bush the bears had missed, and then rinsing my mouth with snow for moisture. The night Mom came to visit, the afternoon was dimming and the wind was changing direction and picking up speed at the same time, making the waning day feel cold, barren and incredibly lonely.

My feet were scratched, cracked and smeared with dried blood from the dry cold and crusty snow. My hands looked more like chapped claws than human fingers. My back and legs ached from staggering through heavy wet snow. I was a mess. I'd spent several minutes that morning massaging my feet. Then, instead of pulling on the socks that were falling apart from slogging through the woods, I slipped the sheepskin mitts over them. It wasn't easy keeping the mitts on, and

I had to basically shuffle on my way, but at least they were waterproof and warm. One of my toes was a scary blue colour and I knew I'd have to keep them dry from now on.

My fears of wild animals, which had bothered me on and off, had disappeared, and were replaced by a strange sort of inertia and a raging thirst. I was hungry, too, although not as hungry as a day or two earlier. Food, I knew, was now my biggest challenge. So far all I'd eaten since leaving camp were dried berries and some rose-hips off the bushes on my trek. I had nothing to use as a snare, and even if I did manage against all odds to catch some little beast for dinner, the matter of how I would handle cooking it when I had no means to start a fire was another question. I wasn't yet hungry enough to view raw mouse casserole with any kind of enthu-siasm, but at the same time I knew I had to eat something.

I pulled the drawstring from the hood of my jacket, laid the little circle of string out with shaking hands and then dusted a light covering of snow over to hide my scent. I tied the other end to a little branch and then, sucking on a handful of snow, I slogged on a little farther to a large tree-fall.

"Bed." I said it aloud just for the comfort of a human voice. "Beddy-boys, time. Man, I could use some sleep."

By the time I pulled down an assortment of pine boughs for use as a mattress any warmth the day had held earlier had disappeared. My stomach was growling, rebel-ling when the melt of chilly snow hit it, and I yanked down a couple more branches and pulled them over me for a rough blanket. Snuggling down into my jacket, I reached out for another fistful of snow. I was incredibly thirsty.

"Deer," I said with a sudden spurt of inspiration. "They eat willow bark. It doesn't kill them. They like it, so it can't be poisonous. Tomorrow I'll hunt down some willow bark," I promised myself. Make some tea. Willow bark tea. I knew it'd be tasty, and in my dreamy delirium I didn't even realize I had no way of actually building a fire, melting snow in a pot and boiling up bark. Still, that hot tea was a comforting thought.

But when morning came I could barely lift my head. The air was cold, the wind vicious as it whipped icy pellets of snow out of the lowering cloud.

Every bone, every muscle, ached. Little flickers of pain tore up through the calves of my legs. The joints throughout my body felt like frozen fire. It felt like

I'd never get warm again. I was freezing, my teeth chattering so hard I was afraid I'd bite through my tongue. At the same time I was sweating like an overheated sauna, the beads of sweat running saltily down into my eyes and soaking the edge of my hat.

Dad had spent many long hours attempting to instill in Jamie and me a healthy fear of hypothermia from exposure, and warned us against being caught out in the elements without proper protection. He and the Aunts were constantly stressing about the body losing heat, and driving home the point that one of the compelling signs of hypothermia is the inability to think rationally. By the time my fever and chills hit I was too confused to know if I was thinking straight or not.

I lay there all that day, too tired and sleepy to do more than suck on a fistful of snow once in a while. The thought of chomping on willow bark, or anything else for that matter, gave a woozy kind of feeling to the experience.

Then Mom came to check me out. It was getting dark again, and she must have realized how lonely I was curled up down there under the pine branches. I'd been talking to myself for company, but it hadn't helped ease the loneliness much, and now I was so stiff with cold I didn't want to move even to reach out for snow. In spite of the cold, part of me was hot; my head under my hat was sweaty and the back of my neck ached like crazy, but it took too much energy to even think about removing my hat. The most I could do was lie there and listen to the wind whine through the branches around me.

The sun was only a sinking yellowish blob behind a light covering of cloud. Cloud that didn't appear soft and moist anymore, but had that cold hard edge that hinted at snow and bitter weather ahead.

"Oh, give me a home," I sang feebly to myself. It was a problem trying to remember the words. "Where the hmmm hmmm do roam . . ."

Mom's face swam gently into view next to mine. She was inches away from me, and at the same time, miles away. She was smiling and her warmth was palpable.

"Hi!" I said goofily. I was thrilled at the sight of another human being. "How ya doin'?"

Her face was strong, her eyes kind and full of humour, and she leaned over me, putting her warm face next to mine, but the hand she held up to stroke my face was a paw. It looked soft, but under the curved pads I knew there would be claws. It was a tawny colour, gold and cream mixed with a dark red-brown.

"Mom," I began, uncertain how to tell her there was something wrong with her hand.

And then she was gone again. All I could see was a broken branch swaying drunkenly in the breeze. Little flakes of snow drifted lazily down around me. The air was fresh and so cold it hurt to breathe.

I huddled further down into my jacket in my makeshift bed. Hugging my arms across my chest, I began to sing again.

"Don't worry, be happy," I warbled. Cold air entering my mouth made me cough and sputter so hard it made my eyes water.

Again Mom's face appeared out of a blast of light dry snow. She smiled and started to speak. Her mouth was open, forming words, but I couldn't hear her.

"Can't hear you!" I hollered over the wind. "Speak up! What're you trying to say? It's cold, Mom, really cold." A sob climbed up my throat and my whole body shuddered with exhaustion and chills.

She smiled at me wordlessly now, then she drew closer. Curving her long cat body around mine, she was a warm, soft vision of creamy gold fur, offering me heat and protection. I was deeply touched by her exposing herself to the frigid wind in order to shield me.

"Mom." I half-sobbed. "Thanks. It's so cold out here. There's no way to get warm. Jamie says we all die of the cold. He says . . ."

"Jamie's OK." Her voice echoed through my head. "Jamie wants you to come back. Come on now, let me help you up."

"OK, Mom."

"Just let me get you on your feet, OK?"

"No!" I was immediately afraid if I stood, she'd leave me alone again. "Mom, listen, it's freezing out here. The snow is so pretty and it's so cold and there's nothing here but trees. Wrap yourself around me again, OK, Mom? Come on, please . . ."

The soft furry body of the huge cat wrapped itself comfortably around my frozen legs, and Mom's face gazed gently into mine. Her eyes were sad. The strength was there and they were filled with a kind of sorrowful love that even now I can't describe or ever forget.

"Come on, Davey," she coaxed. "Let's get warmed up."

Then she was gone again and Thor's tongue was rough against my cheek, rasping away at the cat's image. I found myself on top of a horse with somebody's

arms holding me in place. I wanted to turn and see if I was riding with Mom; I
needed to see her face again, but I was too tired. Bone-deep fatigue lay like a heavy
blanket against me. All I wanted was sleep, deep quiet sleep sucking around the
edges of consciousness, pulling me down. It irritated me that the jolting movements of the horse made that kind of sleep impossible.

The rest of that week is still a blur, but from what I hear from the Aunts it became
very cold. The wind was a demon, and the drama caused by my taking off had
pretty much broken the back of Dad's experiment in the woods. Everything had
changed, including Dad, and he packed us all up and back to our old lives with our
old demons and our old hurts all intact and new ones added. There was no running
away from it all, and both Dad and I found that out the hard way.

Even now, back in school with Jamie being his normal weird self, the Aunts
back in their little house with Lisa, and Dad back to his painting, even now it's
unclear to me how we got back here. The whole experience on my own in those
dramatic woods seems like a dream sometimes. One a person would like to hang
onto, dig a little deeper into, but at the same time one that is almost too intimi-
dating to really look at. Who knows what I might find if I really look at it? When
I remember it I see it mostly in black and white – sharp, angulated branches like
slashes against blinding white snow.

Except for the part about Mom. She's gold and glowing like a sort of orb. I've
told Lisa some of what happened out there in the snow when I met Mom, but it's
hard to put into words. Some of it was more a feeling than an actual experience. It
was a powerful thing to go through, which makes describing it even more difficult.
There's no room for anyone laughing at me or making it sound silly. It was real,
and Lisa, to her credit, lets me talk as much as I want in my efforts to understand
what happened.

There are moments when I'm back out there in the dark, the cold, the bush,
and I can feel movement around me even if I can't see it; moments when everything
is still around me and the things that are solidly in front of my eyes feel more
wispy and insubstantial than the images floating in my head. I remember those
sparks around her, and the intense heat coming from her body and her generosity
in sharing that heat with me when I was bone-cold.

Dad is still quiet about it all. He doesn't talk about our experiences or mention
Mom, so in other words nothing much has changed. He's mostly dedicated to

making Lisa's life a lot easier than it has been, and he's making sure he's part of her life. He takes her to town to shop. He invites her here. He wants the two of us to be friends, and we're working on it. Grudgingly sometimes, but we're trying.

Pete thinks the whole Mom thing was my imagination working overtime. He says seeing Mom as a mountain lion was a trick of the light. I tell him about her warmth and her voice when she was talking to me and he just shrugs.

The Aunts, of course, tell me Mom came over from the other side. They insist that communicating from the other side of dying is hard for those who've died and that we need to be thankful when it happens. They say I'm lucky and they sometimes look at me as if they wonder how I came to be so fortunate when I'm such an obvious doofus in their eyes. They say spirits visit us all the time; it's just we're too busy and too preoccupied to pay attention. The Aunts look at me speculatively, as if they think maybe I've got special powers, as if some of Mom's ancestors might be trying to communicate through me. They seem to expect more from me now. And that might be a problem.

Jamie just laughs whenever we talk about the trip. He says he saw bugs when he was feverish. He had bugs crawling through his legs and up his spine and when he remembers it he shivers dramatically.

Mostly he's thinking and plotting about the cuties he expects to impress at next summer's powwow. He's got some idea of learning to hoop dance. Thinks the hoops, the colours, a feather or two are going to be his ticket to paradise. He scammed an old bent Hula Hoop from a random playground kid in return for obscure future favours, and he's got some red ribbon he wants to glue on it. In Jamie's world it's only one small step from learning to balance a Hula Hoop, to adding one more hoop and then another and another and before you know it he's the hero in the middle of 12 crazy hoops all wound in different directions around his body with the adoring screams of lovely young ladies ringing in his ears.

But sometimes, when he doesn't notice me watching him I see him sit and finally shut up for a while and he seems to be miles away in a different world from this one. And I guess I'm there too sometimes, still trying to make some sort of sense out of what happened. It was a big deal at the time, and it should have some kind of meaning, but life still goes on pretty much like it always did.

The only thing that's really changed is inside me where I'm even less clear about who I am and what I want from my life. And still struggling with what happened to my Mom and how her life turned so bad. But there's always the Aunts. And because I hang with Lisa once in a while now, I'm starting to see the two of them in a slightly different light. They have their own way of living, half in this century and half in an earlier one, partly Aboriginal and partly white, and they just take what they need and leave the rest.

Me, I don't know. I don't think anything. I can't forget what happened and I can't stop it from coming back. Sometimes I could swear she's right there – right beyond what I can see or touch – and sometimes what happened in the dark cold woods seems more real than what I'm doing right now, right here.

All I know for sure is things change. And things don't change. Life's random that way.